All My Beautiful Tomorrows

Murray Pura

MillerWords, LLC
PO Box 1622
Mount Dora, FL 32756

First Edition

For discounts on bulk purchases, please contact MillerWords Educational Sales at **Sales@MillerWords.com**

Printed in the United States of America

2 4 6 8 10 9 7 5 3 1

Library of Congress Control Number: 2017916448

ISBN: 978-0-9982986-9-6

Chapter 1

*H*ey, Smiles. What does a person have to do to get some attention around here?"

Kirsten MacLeod looked up from the German grammar she had been leaning over, metal coffee pot in one hand, and laughed.

"Only one person calls me that and he gets plenty of attention." She smiled at a young man in a green flannel shirt settling onto a stool at the lunch counter. "Hey. I thought you were out of town."

"Got in last night. But I have to take off again in a few hours with a shipment for Chicago."

She put a clean cup by his hand and poured coffee into it. "You really are burning the candle at both ends."

"Only way I know to get my trucking business off the ground. My years in Afghanistan slowed my life down a bit." He sipped at his coffee. "But I don't regret the service to my country one bit. It'll all come together."

1

"I like your spirit, Brandon." Kirsten handed him a plastic-covered menu. "Have to wait on some other customers. I'll be right back."

She went down the counter pouring coffee, taking orders, chatting with customers, and gathering up dirty dishes. When she returned to Brandon, one hand was under his chin and the other was holding the menu the same way he'd been holding it when she left.

"You haven't got far," she said.

"Sure, I have. Coffee's all gone."

She poured him another cup.

"You know we really should be seeing each other more often." Brandon put the menu down.

"We do see each other more often."

"Here in Zook's Diner, sure. Can't we change the scenery?"

"What did you have in mind?"

"A meal somewhere else, maybe even Philly. A movie. A long talk."

"Okay. But it has to be one of the nights I'm not with the Schrock family. So that means Saturday or Sunday."

"Not Friday?"

She shook her head. "Friday doesn't work."

"Okay. Will you go into Philly with me Sunday night?"

"Sure. Can we go in your rig?"

"My rig?" He leaned back on the red vinyl stool and grinned through his sandy brown beard. "You want to go on a date with me into Philly in my rig?"

"Yeah, I do. Is that too much to take in?"

"I can handle it. Just thought you'd prefer my Ford."

She made a face. "I drive around in an old pickup all the time."

"You have a Chevy. My Ford's brand new."

"I don't care. A pickup is a pickup. What's the matter, Brandon Peters? Too much truck for you in the big city?"

"Ha. I pick up shipments in Philly all the time. I'll be at your place at four. Supper, movie, a long coffee and a long talk. The rig will be your limo."

"Promise?"

"I swear." He raised his right hand. "Now that we've got our business out of the way could I trouble you for a cheeseburger and fries, Kirsten MacLeod?"

"You call that breakfast?" She didn't finish writing it down on her pad. "You ordered the same thing the last three times."

He shrugged. "So, I'm predictable."

"Predictable? We'll see."

At four-thirty Kirsten untied her apron, said goodbye to the other waitresses and the chef, and walked out to the gravel parking lot. She was about to slip behind the wheel of her 2000 red and black Chevy pickup when a dark buggy drew up beside her. A particularly beautiful chestnut horse was harnessed to the buggy. The horse had been brushed until it gleamed. She sat a moment, admiring the mare. A tall and slender Amish man stepped down from the buggy, dressed in black despite the early spring heat, though the broad-brimmed hat on his head was straw. He glanced at her but did not smile. His eyes were a sharp blue, so sharp Kirsten felt the gaze make its way right through her. She quickly dropped her eyes and placed her keys in the ignition, but she could not keep herself from looking back. His eyes were still on her. Now there was a faint smile on his lips. After another moment, he walked across the parking lot to the diner. She watched him go inside.

"What was that all about?" she murmured.

Her eyes remained on the screen door with its diagonal red Coca-Cola bar.

"That was great." Kirsten shook her head and started the Chevy pickup. "Really great. Now my life is even more confusing than it was already."

She drove to her house. It was two stories, white, with a small lawn and even smaller rose bushes, but "clean and tight as a yacht", as her father used to say. She came in the door, spent a moment looking at the pictures of three men in uniform on the wall by the hallway mirror, went to her room, changed into a long dark dress with long sleeves, unpinned her brown hair, brushed it out, put it up in a tight bun, and walked back out to the truck. She drove for about twenty minutes, passing six horse-drawn buggies on the way, and stopped in front of a farmhouse that was three stories high and painted a bright white just like her own home.

"Ah, Kirsten, *gut, gut.*" A tall thin woman in a long black dress met her at the door and hugged her. "Malachi is looking for you. His eyes are always on the door."

"Oh, I miss him after a weekend, Lydia. I'm glad he misses me too."

"Of course, he does."

A man taller and heavier than the woman who hugged Kirsten extended his hand. "*Willkommen*. How are you today, young lady?"

"I'm fine, *danke schoen*, Mr. Schrock."

"Not Mr. Schrock. You have been coming to our house for half a year now to bless our boy. Adam, you must call me Adam."

Kirsten smiled and shook his hand. "Very well. It's good to be back in your home, Adam. Is Malachi in the front room?"

"*Ja, ja,* he is just there by the window. You know how he loves the big window."

Kirsten went from the hall into a room that had one couch, one chair, and one table. A young boy in a wheelchair with shining blond hair, the sunlight bathing him, laughed and began to swing his arms and legs and head in a kind of rhythm, his mouth open in a wide smile.

"Malachi!" Kirsten hugged and kissed the boy and mussed his hair. "How was your weekend? Did you miss me?"

The boy grunted and grinned and continued to swing his body from side to side.

"Well, I think we must go outside for our walk. You can see how beautiful an afternoon it is." Kirsten unlocked the wheelchair's brake and began to push Malachi towards the door. Adam held it open. "*Danke schoen*, Adam. You and Lydia can go about your errands in town now."

"*Gut. Danke.*" Adam took a wide-brimmed straw hat off a hook. "We will be back at eight or nine."

"That's fine. You know I will be here until nine. Longer, if necessary."

"His supper is in the ice box." Lydia adjusted the black prayer *kapp* on her head. "Yours too. *Gott segne Sie.*"

"*Danke,*" replied Kirsten. "*Und moge Gott Sie segnen.*"

Adam drove a buggy from the back of the house and reined the horse in. Lydia walked down the wooden ramp from the front door, Adam helped her up into the seat beside him, and soon the buggy was rattling along the road to Intercourse.

"We cannot go as fast as they can, Malachi," said Kirsten as she wheeled him out onto the roadway. "But we can stop and smell the roses."

Malachi swung his head from left to right, smiling.

The right side of his face and body was strong and complete, the way a healthy eleven-year-old boy should look. The left side was withered and shrunken. His left hand was curled in upon itself and frozen in that position. When they stopped for a minute, Kirsten took the frozen hand, rubbed it, opened it up, and massaged all the fingers.

"How is that, Malachi?"

She took his left leg, thin and with very little muscle compared to the right, and massaged it as well. After that she kissed him on the forehead and they continued along the road, sticking to a smooth surface of well-worn dirt at the side and avoiding the stones and gravel in the middle. Twice buggies passed them, their horses stepping briskly, and the drivers waved. Kirsten waved back with one hand while continuing to push with the other.

"Look." Kirsten pointed so that Malachi could see her arm and hand and finger. "There are purple flowers in the ditch. Should I pick some?"

A combination of grunts and gurgles came from his throat. She put the brake on the chair, walked into the grassy ditch, knelt in her long black dress, picked a handful of the small flowers that had no scent, and gave them to Malachi. He put them to his nose again and again. She continued to push the chair. A yellow-breasted meadowlark perched on a fence post and sang out. Malachi swung his body from side to side and used his right hand to push on the right wheel and propel the chair towards the bird. Kirsten took him down into the ditch, although the tall grass made it difficult to move quickly. The meadowlark did not fly. They stayed in the bottom of the ditch and watched the bird for several minutes. Malachi grew still.

"It's my favorite bird," Kirsten whispered. "What do you think, Malachi? Or do you like robins more? Or Canada geese?"

But Malachi remained quiet.

They were on the road almost two hours. When Kirsten rolled Malachi up the sidewalk to his house the robins were just starting their evening songs. She knew he liked the sound so she stopped by an apple tree in the front yard. A robin was on the highest branch and sending out its music. Malachi swung a little bit and then was still once again, his eyes on the male bird with its deep red chest. Another male began to sing from the top of a tool shed at the side of the house. The air filled with their summer evening calls.

"So, it is good to be alive." Kirsten kissed Malachi on the top of the head. "Now we should go inside and get something to eat."

Wednesday evening, the bishop's house, near the Schrock's home, 8:45 PM

"Amen, amen, amen."

Bishop Yoder finished his prayer in High German and sat back down at the kitchen table.

"Amen, amen, amen." Three ministers voiced the words in unison, their heads still bowed.

"Amen." Kirsten lifted her face and waited.

The three gray-bearded men sat across the round wooden table from her.

The bishop had one hand in his beard, tugging, while the other held a sheet of paper.

"You are finished for the night at the Schrocks, *ja*?" he asked Kirsten without looking up.

"Yes, sir."

"And it is every evening, Monday to Friday, you have volunteered to help them with Malachi? Eden Health Services employs you?"

"Well, yes, but there is no money involved other than a payment of gas for my truck."

"Gasoline. Hm." The bishop's fingers left his beard and tapped on the table. "The Schrocks speak well of you. How do you get along with the boy?"

"I adore him, sir. He is so fresh and excited by life."

"The cerebral palsy was a great blow to them when he was born."

"The umbilical cord was wrapped around his neck. There should have been a Caesarean section. It cut off . . ."

The bishop held up his free hand. "It is what it is. God's will."

Kirsten did not reply.

The bishop kept on reading, not making eye contact with her. "Your father served in the army in the Gulf War. Also, your brother. In Iraq."

"Yes, sir. Two different wars."

"Both were killed. I am sorry."

"Thank you."

"A fiancé was also in uniform, hmm?"

"Sergeant Ty Samson. He was a Marine."

"They do not know what happened to him?"

"He was –" Kirsten stopped and took a breath, looking down. "He was listed as KIA in Afghanistan more than two years ago, sir. I have not heard anything more since the official letter I received. They never brought his body home. They never found it."

The bishop drummed his fingers. "Your mother passed away five or six years ago."

"Yes, sir. Cancer."

"Once again, I am sorry." He put down the sheet of paper and looked at her. "You have had more than your share of trials and tribulations. Yet it has not diminished your faith in God."

"No, sir."

"We like to think such times bring us closer to him because we must rely on him much more."

"I suppose that's true for me, sir. I really have had nowhere else to turn but him."

"You attend a church in Lancaster?"

"Yes. Our family church. But I do not feel comfortable there anymore. I find it difficult to speak about what I have gone through. I feel people do not wish to hear about it. A number of them have lost brothers and sons too so they would rather not keep bringing it up, even for prayer."

"Is that why you want to join the Amish? To make the talk? You understand we would not discuss the terrors of war either?"

"I would join the Amish to chat?" Kirsten shook her head. "I would join so I could have people to talk to? No, I would become one with you because I believe in your way of faith. That is why I request permission to take classes and be baptized. Of course, I have seen the Amish people since I was a little girl. But working with the Schrocks I have grown much closer to you all. I have thought about this, prayed about it, this is a step I feel led to take."

One of the ministers leaned forward. "You have talked about this with Adam Schrock and his wife?"

"Yes."

"They support this idea of yours?"

"Yes, sir, but I hope it is not simply an idea of mine. I hope I am following God's call when I ask you to consider bringing me into your community."

Another minister spoke up. "The Yoder Amish are not so lenient as other groups. Our way is very narrow. *Strait is the gate and narrow is the way which leadeth unto life and few there be that find it.* Are you sure this what you are called to?"

"Yes."

"You would marry within our people? Raise your children among us?"

She nodded. "I would."

The third minster lifted his hands, palms upward. "If only it were so easy. You say yes, we say yes, life is perfect. But there are a number of matters to consider. The most important one is your family history."

"What about my family history, sir?"

"Come, come."

He was the skinniest of the men. Kirsten thought he looked almost skeletal. It made her more anxious than she already felt as she sat in the kitchen with the four older men.

"You want to be one with our people," the minister went on. "So, you understand what we believe. We do not wage war. We do not enlist. Nowhere will you find a flag flying from our houses or barns. It is not for us to harm others. *Thou shalt not kill.*"

"I know that."

"But look at your family. Your father was a soldier. Your brother was a soldier. Your fiancé was a soldier. God have mercy on their souls. May I ask about your grandfather?"

"On my mother's side or my father's?"

"Both. Were they soldiers? Did they fight?"

"One of them did, yes. Grandfather MacLeod flew an airplane in World War Two."

"You see? It is all through your family, from one generation to the next. It is not so with the Yoder Amish or any of the other Amish. We do not raise soldiers. There are no pilots among us." The skinny minister looked at the other men. "I cannot see it. Before God, I cannot see her taking instruction and being baptized into the faith."

The bishop leaned his head to one side. "Well, but she does a great work of compassion for the Schrock family. With them it as if she were the hands of Christ."

The skinny minister agreed. "*Ja*, this is good, we all understand that, Bishop Yoder. She is welcome among us to serve the Schrock family and care for young Malachi. But all this warfare! A family history soaked in violence and bloodshed! Can we unite this to the Yoder Amish?

Can we call it good and accept it? Do we tell our people it is all right? Never. Never."

The minister next to him looked at Kirsten. "Pastor Gore is right. You do good among us. But you would not bring good among us. Even if we baptized you a hundred times over."

Bishop Yoder interlaced his fingers and rested both hands on the tabletop. "But here is a question for you, Miss MacLeod. Do you honor what your father and brother have done, what your grandfather did? Did the government give you medals for the fighting they engaged in? Do you keep those medals in a special place? A box, a drawer?"

Kirsten's body went cold. "There were some medals."

"Have you kept them?"

"I would not throw them out. I could never do that."

"Do you honor your family members for the killing they did? Do you thank God for the warfare they waged on others? Against the German people and the Middle Eastern people?"

"I would not put it that way."

"How would you put it?"

"They fought for America. To keep us free. To keep you free. Would the Amish like to live in a country ruled by Adolf Hitler? Would Hitler have granted the Amish the liberty to practice their Christian faith as they wished? Isn't that why your ancestors left Europe to begin with, Bishop Yoder? Weren't they persecuted by people just as bad as the Nazis?"

The bishop waved his hands in the air. "We are not here to argue or debate. What others feel they must do before God is up to them. They will have to give an answer on the Day of Judgment. For ourselves, we do not shed blood, we can never shed blood, nor can we honor those who do. Or honor those who honor the way of the soldier." He folded the sheet of paper with Kirsten's information on it in half, then in half again. "My girl, there is no place for you here. To help Malachi is one thing. To remain grateful for what the soldiers in your family have done is something else." He glanced at the ministers sitting beside him at the table. "Are we agreed?"

The three ministers nodded.

"I am sorry, Miss MacLeod." The bishop folded the sheet of paper a third time. "You may walk with God as you feel you ought. But you cannot walk with us. Pastor Gore, please close our session in prayer."

The skinny pastor got to his feet. "Let us pray, brothers."

Kirsten hardly heard the prayer. Balling her hands into fists, struggling to keep back the tears, she kept her head bowed while Pastor Gore prayed. As soon as they each pronounced their amens, she thanked them and was out of the kitchen and out of the house through the back door. She stumbled in the dark, got to the roadway where her 2000 Chevy was parked, climbed in, and started the truck. But she pressed the gas pedal down too long and flooded the engine. She kept twisting the key in the ignition but the pickup refused to start. Leaning her head against the steering wheel she began to cry.

"Hey, hey, what is this?" A young man appeared at her open window. "Are you hurt, *Fraulein?*"

Kirsten did not even lift her head or look at him. "I'm all right, I'm not hurt, please go away."

"But why are you crying?"

"I don't know. It doesn't matter. My truck won't start."

"Perhaps I can help."

Kirsten glanced up, tears racing over her cheeks. "You're Amish."

"*Ja,* I am Yoder Amish."

"What would you know about cars and trucks?"

"I am the blacksmith. Also, the farrier."

Kirsten stared at him. It was the young man she had seen in the parking lot of the diner, the one whose buggy had been pulled by a beautiful chestnut horse. The man who had looked at her with his brilliant blue eyes.

"Blacksmith?" repeated Kirsten. "Farrier? Do you think my Chevy needs a wagon wheel? Or a set of horseshoes?"

The young man smiled a gentle smile. "Well, I have a way with things. So, I can smell the gasoline. You must wait a few minutes. You have flooded the engine. Next time you try to start it do not press down so much on the gas pedal. It will start all right then."

"How do you know?" Kirsten had stopped crying.

"Oh, I see things among the English in Lancaster, I hear things."

"I hope you're right."

"Let's find out. Now . . . turn the key, tap the gas pedal with your foot, just tap it."

The engine roared to life.

Kirsten began to laugh. "It's like magic."

"Not magic. Sometimes it is best to go about things easy."

"Easy. I will try and remember that."

"So, what is your name?" he asked.

"Kirsten MacLeod. How about you?"

"Joshua Miller. Tell me, what brings you to the bishop's house?"

The laughter left Kirsten's face. "Oh, it doesn't matter. I spoke with him about a matter and now it is all over."

"All over?"

"Yes, finished, *kaput*." She released her parking brake. "I must go. Thank you so much for your help. *Danke schoen*."

"Wait. I know who you are. The young woman, the *Englisch* nurse."

"I'm no nurse. Just a waitress."

"But it's you who help the Schrocks with Malachi, *ja*? I am certain it is you."

"How can you be so certain?"

"*Ach*, it is – it is the way you are. Your hair color, the way you walk, and, of course, I recognize your truck."

"The way I walk?"

Kirsten could have sworn she saw the young man blush as he stood in the roadway in the dark.

He removed his straw hat from his head. "I did not mean to offend. Forgive me."

"You didn't offend. My goodness. It's nice to be noticed in this busy world." She smiled. "Now you have me feeling better again. But I really must go."

"*Ja, ja*, of course. I hope I see you again."

"Well, if you see the Chevy you'll know I'm around. Say, do you like coffee, Mr. Miller?"

"Coffee? *Ja*, sure, I drink it all the time."

"Next time you are free drop by Zook's Diner. You have a coffee waiting for you there. I'll pour it personally. My way of thanking you for giving me a hand tonight."

"Zook's? I'll be there tomorrow morning."

She laughed. "Just like that? I thought the Amish were slow. You don't let any grass grow under your feet, do you?"

His gentle smile. "I try not to. There is always somewhere to go and another job to do."

"Well, make your way to Zook's Diner tomorrow, okay? Make that one of your jobs."

"I will. *Danke*, Miss Macleod."

"*Bitte,* Mr. Miller."

She drove off down the road under a crescent moon and Joshua watched her go, not moving, his straw hat still in his hands.

Chapter 2

April
Wednesday night,
Kirsten Macleod's house, 11:00 PM

Alone in her bedroom, Kirsten cried until she felt she had nothing left inside her.

The Schrocks had been praying for her. They had been so confident of a good outcome and had wanted Kirsten to drop by after her meeting with the bishop and ministers. But she had not been able to do it. She had headed straight home after her trouble with the Chevy.

Coming in through the door she had spent several minutes looking at the photographs of her father and brother and fiancé. Finally, fresh tears darting down her face, she had touched her father's picture with her fingertips.

"I could never turn my back on you, dad," she whispered. "Not on any of you. I am not ashamed. I'm proud. I love you."

Now she sat on the edge of her bed in her cotton nightgown and read from her Bible, balled up tissue in one hand. A candle gave the only light in the room. At bedtime Kirsten liked to pretend she was Amish.

Peace I leave with you, my peace I give unto you. Not as the world giveth, give I unto you. Let not your heart be troubled, neither let it be afraid.

She flipped to another page she had bookmarked.

I have told you these things, so that in me you may have peace. In this world, you will have trouble. But take heart! I have overcome the world.

She gazed at the candle flame. It burned perfectly tall and straight and golden.

"I should be like you," she said. "No wavering. No growing dark. Light, and bright, and steady, and the color of purest gold. Perhaps someday."

She laid her head back on her pillow.

"Why did I believe what my family had done in the military wouldn't matter? What was I thinking? Oh, Lord, I should never have started this whole Amish business. But now I'm too attached to the Schrocks and Malachi to quit. They'll probably talk me into approaching the bishop for a second meeting. But what can I say, Lord? Nothing will have changed. I am not going to disown my father and brother." She turned her head and looked at the photograph of a dark-eyed and smiling young man in the dress uniform of a Marine. "And I'm certainly not going to disown you, Ty. I love you. I miss you. I guess you're gone. But to me you'll always be around one way or another. I hope you don't mind that I'm going to go to a movie with Brandon. I have to do something. I'm all alone. It hurts so much. I'm starting to feel like this old unwanted woman of twenty-two. I even get backaches now. Maybe I'm on my feet too much."

Kirsten propped herself on one elbow, blew Ty a kiss, and blew out the candle with the same breath.

She had been having trouble falling asleep and hoped this wouldn't be another difficult night.

I'm bone tired. I should sleep like a log.

But she didn't.

She went over the meeting again and again.

I should have said something else when he asked me about the family church here in Lancaster.

I did not even tell them that others, besides the Schrock family, were in complete agreement with me being baptized into the Amish faith.

Perhaps they do not think I am sincere when I talk about marrying among the Amish.

Joshua Miller's face filled her mind.

She groaned.

"Yes, Mr. Miller," she mumbled in the dark, "you were very kind and you have a handsome face and a handsome smile. Yes, and the good strong body of a blacksmith. But Brandon Peters is enough to worry about. I don't need to have you on my mind as well, I honestly don't."

His face would not go away.

"I am going to go to sleep. Do you understand? You will not be able to follow me there. I will not dream about you. I have no intention at all of ever dreaming about you. So, go look for a bright, young, cheery-eyed Amish girl with blond hair and blue eyes. I'm an old maid. Possibly older than you. *Guten nacht. Auf wiedersehen.*"

Very little changed after her declaration and command except Brandon's face hovered into view and finally Ty's.

Even though her eyes were closed she slapped the back of her arm over her face.

"I am drinking too much coffee. That is why I am not sleeping well these days. Starting tomorrow, no more coffee, not even half a cup."

Saying this made her remember she had invited Joshua Miller to Zook's Diner for a coffee.

We never set a date. I left it open-ended. Yes, yes, we said tomorrow, but he'll forget about it. He won't come. I know he won't come. I am English – eine Fraulein Englisch. And I don't need any more troubles than I already have.

But Joshua was there the moment she started her shift at six-thirty the next morning. The diner opened at six, but he was sitting in his buggy when she drove up and parked, and he did not enter until she was behind the counter in her apron and pale yellow uniform. He took off his wide-brimmed straw hat and sat on a red stool at the counter.

"*Guten Morgen,*" he greeted her.

The diner was already noisy with truckers and farmers, but his quiet voice carried through the loud conversations, and the clash of knives and forks and plates, like an arrow.

She covered her surprise with a smile she realized was far too large and bright for him or for the moment. "*Guten Morgen, Herr Miller.*"

Her full smile widened his. "How are you? Is your Chevrolet well?"

"My Chevrolet?" She poured him a cup of coffee. "Oh, of course, it's fine, it started perfectly this morning. Well, there is your coffee, it's on the house, thank you for all your help last night."

Joshua lifted the cup to his mouth. Curls of steam covered his face. "So, I will need some food today. I have pickup trucks to put buggy wheels on and there are many Chevys and Fords to shoe."

Kirsten had turned to get a menu for a customer sitting two stools down from Joshua. "What?" She looked back at Joshua. Then she laughed. "Mr. Miller, are you pulling my leg?"

"Horses' legs. I only pull horses' legs."

She put one hand on her hip. The other was holding a pot of coffee. She told herself not to grin, but she grinned anyways.

"Mr. Miller. I can't recall the other Amish I've met being quite as lively as you are this morning."

"I am always lively in the mornings. And afternoons. Evenings too can find me lively."

"So, when do you settle down?"

"When my head hits the pillow. Then I am out like a light."

She left to take an order from a truck driver at the end of the counter. When she returned his cup was empty so she refilled it.

"Are you going to eat?" she asked him. "Or is it just the free coffee?"

"I like free, sure. But I'm happy to pay for a plate of bacon and eggs and sausages and *Pfannkuchen*."

"Sounds like you want the Hearty Man Breakfast. That's a lot of food."

He shrugged. "I have a lot of work to do. Shoeing Chevys, hammering wagon wheels onto Fords, maybe a plow for seeding time for the Dodge Ram."

She laughed again and the men in the diner all looked at her. Noticing that, her hand went to her mouth.

"I'm too loud," she said. "Everyone is looking."

Joshua sipped his fresh cup of coffee. "That is not why they are looking."

"No?" Kirsten picked up an order and moved swiftly down the counter to a man with a battered cowboy hat on his head. "Here you are, Mr. Stearman." She came back to Joshua. "So why are they looking, Mr. Miller?"

Part of her felt she should not ask the question. Another part of her was sure he wouldn't answer. Yet another part felt reckless and she hoped he would be a bit reckless too, even if he were Amish.

Joshua continued to sip his coffee.

She sensed that he too was deciding what he should say or not say, weighing the consequences, stalling as he made up his mind whether to be careful or careless.

A decision came into his eyes and she knew immediately what he was going to tell her.

She felt she ought to stop him, but she didn't open her mouth. Instead a flush began to slip up from her neck onto her cheeks.

"They look at you because you are beautiful." Joshua seemed to blush too. "Excuse me. I do not wish to offend."

At first, Kirsten did not respond.

The cook told her a plate of waffles was ready, and she picked it up, and took it to the trucker at the far end of the counter.

When she returned Joshua was standing and putting his hat on his head.

"You ordered a Hearty Man Breakfast," she protested.

"Ah, I must go, I'm sorry, pardon me."

"But I've placed the order."

"*Ja, ja,* I apologize, I must get to the smithy." He put a ten-dollar bill on the counter. "Perhaps someone else needs the breakfast more than I."

"The meal's only 6.95, Mr. Milller."

"Well, the rest is a tip, *danke, danke.* I wish you a good day, Miss MacLeod."

"Excuse me, Mr. Miller." For a moment, her tone was sharp. "MR. MILLER."

People kept eating but dozens of pairs of eyes fastened on the two of them.

Joshua was halfway to the door. He looked back at Kirsten. "*Ja?*"

"Thank you. That was very sweet of you to say to me. That I am – well, you know. That was very sweet."

He hesitated. "Do you think so?"

"Very much. My day is better because of your kindness. Please come back and eat your breakfast. I wouldn't want to hear that the Amish blacksmith had fainted at his anvil when I visit the Schrocks this afternoon."

He remained standing where he was.

"No, that would not be good," he finally replied.

He walked back to the stool, removed his hat, and sat down.

"Fresh coffee?" she asked.

"Please."

"I'll get you a new cup. No one wants hot coffee on top of cold coffee."

"Thank you, Miss Macleod."

"I think that should stop too, don't you? I'm Kirsten, the waitress who flooded her engine."

He smiled. "So, and I am Joshua, the blacksmith who shoes Chevys."

She laughed her loud laugh again.

He put the new cup of coffee to his lips. "Do you think Malachi would like to see the forge? Would his parents agree to that?" He lifted one shoulder in a shrug. "I don't know if such a sight would please him."

Kirsten ignored the cook who was holding a plate out to her from the serving window of the kitchen.

"I think it would please him a great deal, Joshua. I'll ask his mother and father, but I don't think it will be a problem. Do you want us to meet you at your shop?"

"So, you will come? Just like that?"

"Yes, I will come. Just like that. Malachi will be delighted."

"And you? You also? You will be delighted? A little?"

She grinned, hand on her hip. "A little."

"I come to get you. I will bring my horse and buggy. Five o'clock. All right?"

Kirsten picked up the plate of food the cook had left on the serving shelf. "A perfect time." She placed the meal in front of him. "Hearty Man Breakfast. Are you still hungry?"

He grinned, his blue eyes full of light. "I find I have even more of an appetite now."

"Well, that's good to hear." She began to wipe down the countertop with a damp cloth. "Eat up."

She made her way along the counter, rubbing vigorously as she went.

Kirsten Macleod, she reprimanded herself. *What are you getting yourself into now? You'd better haul back on those reins.*

"Too late," she muttered out loud. "And I don't care either. I really don't."

Thursday evening, Joshua Miller's forge, 5:30 PM

As pleasant as it was to see Joshua's forge, and watch him hammer at a strip of red-hot iron, his large muscles moving along his chest and arms underneath his stained white shirt, Kirsten found herself far more interested in watching the reaction on Malachi's face.

The colors of the sparks glittered in the boy's eyes. The light of the flames leaped about on his face. He did not fidget or squirm or even do his happy dance as he sat in his wheelchair. He sat transfixed, eyes wide, lips parted, watching the fire, watching the smoke, watching the shadows, watching Joshua.

And the noise! The hammer pounding on the hot iron, the bellows whooshing, and fanning the flames, and making them crackle, the loud hiss when Joshua plunged the metal into a large vat of water!

Kirsten laughed out loud, putting the back of her hand to her mouth, watching Malachi begin to grin after several long minutes of dumbfounded silence.

Joshua glanced up at her as he worked, smiling back with an unsure smile at her laughter.

"He loves noise!" she called to him. "Malachi loves lots of noise!"

Now Joshua laughed. "So, he has come to the right place."

At his house, Kirsten often helped Malachi build a tower of empty soup cans and stainless steel bowls, then they would roll baseballs into it until it came crashing down. Malachi would throw his head back, and laugh, and swing his arms in sheer delight.

"I will be done with this wheel rim in a minute," said Joshua, putting aside his hammer. "You must eat with my family, Miss MacLeod."

Kirsten smiled and shook her head. "Oh, no thank you, Joshua. His parents always leave supper for us."

"And it's in the icebox?"

"Yes."

"So, if it's in the icebox today it can be in the icebox tomorrow. And save Mrs. Schrock from making another meal for the pair of you on Friday. Come. I insist. What am I saying? My mother insists. She is dying to meet the famous Kirsten MacLeod."

"Famous?"

Joshua had eight brothers and sisters ranging in age from seven to nineteen – the nineteen-year-old was his brother, Caleb. Joshua, as Kirsten discovered during the course of the meal, was twenty-three, Mrs. Miller's first born. It was a warm and friendly table, but at first the children were not speaking at all because they had not been spoken to, which Kirsten rectified by talking to each of them in turn, so that soon they were as lively as schoolchildren at recess. Plates of ham, scalloped potato, blood sausage, and fresh greens were passed up and down the long table, while Mrs. Miller peppered Kirsten with questions, in-between the questions the children were firing as swiftly as their mother. Mr. Miller shook his head and laughed to himself as he concentrated on his food.

"Such a *ferhoodle*," he said between mouthfuls. "A hundred conversations going on at once and our *Englisch* guest smack in the middle.

It is like she is playing ping pong with all of us at once."

Kirsten spooned food slowly and carefully into Malachi's mouth. "It was thoughtful of you to puree the ham and potatoes ahead of time, Mrs. Miller."

"Oh, we always do it at our church meals. It is my pleasure to see Malachi eat with everyone else. And such a good appetite."

"He does have a good appetite," Kirsten agreed. "It must be the excitement of the forge."

"In a couple of weeks, I am shoeing horses and trimming their hooves," Joshua spoke up. "Is Malachi afraid of horses?"

Kirsten smiled, wiping Malachi's mouth with a cloth napkin. "Not at all."

"Then perhaps you would like to bring him to watch Joshua the Farrier instead of Joshua the Blacksmith?"

"Oh, I'm sure he wouldn't mind seeing Joshua the Blacksmith again. Especially if you keep using that big hammer of yours. The more noise the merrier so far as Malachi is concerned."

"So, you will come again when I am the good Amish farrier?"

"Sure. But only if I can bring something to help with dinner."

Mrs. Miller waved her hand dismissively. "*Ach,* it is no difference to feed ten or eleven or twenty. An army is an army."

"I have to bring something, Mrs. Miller."

"Malachi. Yourself. We don't need anything more than that."

"Still."

The wave of the hand. "As God directs your steps. But it is not for soldiers to cook their own food."

"And am I a soldier, Mrs. Miller?"

The older woman, tall and erect in her chair, did not allow a smile to crease her handsome features. "Of the Lord and his mercies, yes."

Kirsten put down the spoon she was using to feed Malachi. "How is that true?"

"Your love for the broken and the broken-hearted. Not everyone can do that even if their faith in God is strong. I suppose I should not say this, but you belong among us. I know the bishop has spoken against your baptism. But I am certain God would have you among us."

Mr. Miller looked at his ten-year-old daughter Rebecca. "You can bring me the milk and cream, dear."

"*Ja*, Papa."

"Our guest may wish a cup of coffee before Joshua takes her home."

"Just one cup." Kirsten smiled. "Thank you, Mr. Miller."

Mrs. Miller got to her feet. "There are the squares to go with that. Sarah. Tabitha. Please help me, *ja*?"

The subject of Kirsten's attempt to join the Amish faith did not surface again. Or her work with Malachi and the Schrock family and Eden Health Services. Instead they reminisced about her father and her brother and mother. She didn't mind. There were very few people who talked with her about her family. She supposed many thought it hurt her to remember. In one way, it did. But in another way, it was a good hurt.

The Millers remembered her parents and her brother even though neither family had been close to the other. Kirsten could not place the Millers at all in her memories, but she appreciated their stories about how her father had served the Amish community by means of his large hardware store. Or how her mother had helped so many out with her seamstress skills. As if the Amish women needed help there. But for whatever reasons, her mother's abilities had been well respected, and she had been called upon more often than Kirsten could count. Kirsten had only been twelve when the cancer first began to slow her mother down and the disease soon claimed almost all the memories Kirsten had of her – sickly, growing weaker, losing weight, one day unable to rise from bed, her room smelling of the unpleasant scents of decay and inevitable death. It was nice to be offered other people's memories of her mother, memories that were full of life, and of kindnesses given and received. It was like taking dead roses from a vase and replacing them with ones just cut. Or placing a rose bush in a pot in the sunniest room in the house and deciding to do away with dead or dying roses altogether.

There was scarcely any talk on the buggy ride home. Malachi snuggled into her arms, and slept, and the sun dropped into a vivid mix of purple and bronze. There was the *clop-clop* of the horse's metal shoes and once in a while the clicking of Joshua's tongue. When the lamps of the Schrock home appeared, Joshua glanced over at her.

"A good visit," he said softly.

She nodded. "It was."

"It strikes me that you must have to pick him up and carry him a good deal."

"Yes."

"Without any help."

"I can manage." She smiled at him. "You're not the only one with muscles."

Abruptly, he changed the subject. "You understand it has always been this way. Always. No one will change it."

She frowned. "What are you talking about, Joshua?"

"It cannot be altered. You understand? It is such a great part of who we are. Just as you have your President and Congress and Senate."

"Joshua . . ."

"The bishop. Always the bishop has the say. Phone? No phone? The bishop. How long the dresses? What colors? The bishop. Will there be an airplane? Will there not be an airplane? Can buggy wheels have rubber rims instead of iron? The bishop."

Kirsten noisily expelled air from her mouth. "I know, Joshua. I have accepted it. Don't worry."

"But I do worry. Because my family and the Schrocks have not accepted it. Why do you?"

"I . . . I have no other choice."

"You can fight it. You can pray and so you can fight it. Were not your father and brother fighters? Why aren't you? Especially now that you can fight for something that is right. Unlike them."

Kirsten felt cold inside, as if she had swallowed a glassful of ice water too quickly.

Her speech became short and sharp.

Like a pair of scissors cutting paper or fabric. Or string.

"Thank you, Joshua. I can walk from here."

"But the house is . . ."

"Stop the carriage, *bitte*. I can walk with Malachi from here."

Joshua reined in the horse.

Kirsten stepped down, holding Malachi in her arms. *"Danke."*

At her own house, she took a long shower, leaning both hands against the wall, then sat by the big radio her grandfather had purchased in 1942, just before he left for the war, and she listened to music. Or half-listened. One part of her mind drifted with the songs while the other half mulled over the forcefulness of both Mrs. Miller and her son Joshua. She was not used to it from the Amish and certainly not used to them using military metaphors to get across their spiritual points. Nor had she expected Joshua to outright insult the legacy of her father and brother and fiancé by telling her to fight for what was right, *unlike what they had done*. But was that any different from the way Bishop Yoder and Pastor Gore and the others had spoken to her?

"So now tell me, God, yes, God and all the Amish," she said out loud to her empty house, "why should I fight to join the Yoder Amish? Why should I make a second effort to get the bishop to accept me and welcome me in? If the Amish despise my family so much, what is the point of pursuing this dream of mine any longer? It was an illusion, wasn't it, rather than a dream? It had no basis in any kind of reality anywhere."

When she climbed into bed she pulled the covers over her head.

"I am shutting out the Amish except for Malachi and his parents," she whispered. "And that means you too, Joshua the Blacksmith, manly as you are. I need a holiday from all things Amish and all attitudes that are set against soldiers. Would it suit you if we were all wearing swastikas now? Or we were ruled by ISIS? Do you honestly think they would let you remain Amish and enjoy freedom of religion?"

Finally, she peeled the blankets back and took in a great breath of air. "Thank goodness there are truck drivers as well as buggy drivers."

Chapter 3

ᴸooking at stars can be like looking at clouds," Kirsten said, leaning her head back against her seat in the semi and glancing out the open window.

Brandon smiled over at her from the driver's seat. "How's that?"

"You know. How clouds take shapes. That one's a lion, the other one's a horse, the fat one is Mrs. Podiddlyhop." She giggled.

Brandon's smile turned quickly into a grin. "Who is Mrs. Podiddlyhop?"

"Never mind." Kirsten giggled again.

"There never was a Mrs. Podiddlyhop."

"Yes, there was. Yes, there is. And she's just like that group of stars there."

"Huh." Brandon grunted. "Somehow I think those stars have another name."

"Not to me, they don't."

"We had a guy in our squad over in the Sandbox. Called him Professor. Because he knew everything. He'd use a flashlight beam to point

37

out the different constellations. I used to know them all. But tonight, I can't tell you who Mrs. Podiddlyhop really is."

"Tell me about the Sandbox then," asked Kirsten, still gazing out the window. "It's our fourth date and you haven't told me a thing."

"Tell you what about the Sandbox," Brandon responded.

"Anything. Everything."

"Hey. Are you sure you don't want your window up?"

"I'm sure. It's mild enough for me. Do you need a blanket?"

"Ha." Brandon slid down in his seat. "The Sandbox looks like Arizona. It looks a lot like Arizona."

"Well, you'll have to do better than that, Brandon Peters. I've never been to Arizona. I've never been anywhere except Pennsylvania."

"Arizona has all this rugged desert. Tucson is about 2000 feet above sea level, Phoenix 1000, low enough to suck in the heat and cook you like a chicken, but there are lots of mountains too. Brown, amber, purple and blue in the distance, I swear they look like some of the peaks in the Stan . . . you know, Afghanistan. And the Stan can look like northern Arizona too, like around Flagstaff, or like parts of Colorado. It can be really beautiful, big peaks, and these incredible dawns when the sun is some amazing orange you picked in Sarasota or St. Pete's." He laughed. "Other times it can look just like a gravel pit."

Kirsten didn't laugh. "They gave you a purple heart."

Brandon didn't reply.

"And a Navy Cross," Kirsten added.

Silence.

"Okay," he finally said.

"What happened?"

"How do you know all that?" he asked her.

"People at the diner talk. They talk about everything."

"I'm not even from Lancaster."

"They know anyways."

She turned away from the window and the stars to look at his rugged and handsome face with its neatly trimmed beard.

"I feel kinda awkward talking when you've lost a brother in Iraq and your dad before that in the Gulf."

"It's okay."

"And Ty."

"I said it's okay, Brandon."

"We met, you know. I knew him."

"What?"

"In Kandahar."

"How did . . . what did . . . wh . . . what ..." Kirsten stammered.

"We were both from Lancaster County. So, we hung out a few times in the mess. Sergeant Samson. I was part of the rescue. He was still alive when we got to his unit."

Kirsten's eyes were wide in the dark of the semi and riveted on Brandon. "Did you . . .?"

"Yeah. Yeah. I got a chance to talk to him. Just for a sec. Grabbed his hand. Told him it was Brandon from Lancaster. He recognized me. I told him he was gonna be all right. And he was gonna be all right, you know. They stopped the bleeding. Loaded him on the chopper."

"And the chopper got clear."

"Yeah, the dust off got clear."

"But it never made it to back to Kandahar. That's what I was told. The chopper was hit by an RPG. It never made it back."

"No. I guess we kinda hoped it went to another base or had to land in the desert and they all survived."

Kirsten's eyes were glistening. "But that was two years ago and if they'd made it . . ."

Brandon shrugged. "Maybe he's a POW. Maybe friendly tribesmen took him and the others in after the chopper went down. Maybe they're still fighting against the Taliban."

"And they never had a chance to get back to Kandahar in all that time?"

"Maybe he can't be moved. Maybe he's still recovering."

"Brandon . . ."

"Who knows what's possible? We used to say there was this guy, Mahmood Ali, who had a small army he roamed the desert with, offing Taliban, you know, wiping them all out. He hated them. Wanted a good Islamic state like Egypt or Jordan, one without the radicals. So, whenever somebody went MIA we'd say, 'It's okay. Mahmood Ali saved him. He's fighting beside

Mahmood. She's fighting beside Mahmood. We'll see them again soon. They're eating rice and goat meat with Mahmood.'"

"Is that . . . is that what you really think happened to my fiancé? You think Ty might be fighting in Mahmood Ali's desert army?"

"Anything's possible. It's a crazy war in that overseas Arizona. Who knows?"

They were both quiet.

Brandon made a motion with his head. "The North Star. Ursa Major. Ursa Minor."

She gave him a small smile in the dark, but her eyes were wet. "Those I know."

"It was because of that rescue I won the Navy Cross. We took heavy fire saving Ty's unit. Lost three guys from my squad. There was a sniper had us pinned. A couple of them actually. I got around behind them and took them both out. Had to fight my way through a bunch of Taliban to get the snipers. All our choppers got away with the wounded. That's why."

"Thank you," Kirsten said quietly.

For a minute, no one spoke.

"And the purple heart?" she finally asked a second time.

"I don't like talking about myself."

"I just want to know. And then . . . we can talk about something else."

"It was an IED. Blew our armored vehicle wide open. One other guy survived besides me. I lost a lot of muscle in my left arm. It's pretty good now. Not as strong as my right arm. Yet. I make it do the same dumbbell curls as my right arm.

Same weights. Same repetitions. The only easy day was yesterday."

She gave him another smile. "That's the SEALs' motto."

"You're right. I need a better one for the Marines. The only easy day was the day before I joined the Corps. How's that?"

"That's good."

"So that's what I tell my left arm. *Get big or go home* also works."

Kirsten laughed. "I'm sure." She reached out, unsure of herself, hesitant, but finally touched his hand. "May I see it?"

"There's not much to see. My bicep isn't normal on the left arm. It's been pushed up to the shoulder. I'm no longer symmetrical. If I pose and flex, there's no Arnold there."

She shook her head. "I don't care about Arnold."

"You're really serious about this?"

"I am."

"Military brat."

"I am that too."

Brandon rolled up the sleeve of his plaid shirt. "See?"

She leaned towards him. "I can't see anything."

He turned towards her and showed her his bare arm. "There. See how it's pretty flat when I bend my elbow? The muscle's up at the top, not where it's supposed to be."

"It still looks strong. And you have a vein."

"Like I said, I work it hard. My body knows all about that. So, the vein works hard too and brings in the fuel."

"There's a scar." Kirsten reached out with her fingers, hesitated like she had before touching his hand, but finally traced the scar. "It's long."

"Yeah."

She could feel him quivering a bit under her fingertips. "Does it . . . does it hurt?"

"No."

She kept running her fingers up and down his scar and over the flat skin where his bicep should have been. "Thank you for being brave. And thank you . . . for helping Ty."

Brandon nodded.

Her eyes were locked on his, their faces only inches apart, as she continued to trace her fingers over his arm.

"You don't really think there's a Mahmood Ali, do you?" she asked him.

"Well, he's like an idea . . . like a dream or a hope . . . or a prayer . . . or something."

"You don't really think Ty's fighting beside Mahmood."

"Kirsten . . ."

"Or dipping his hand into a bowl of rice and goat meat."

"Crazier things have happened in this crazy world."

"You think Ty's dead, don't you? KIA. Like they told me."

"Really, Kirsten, I try hard not to think about things like that. I try hard not to refight that war every day after I wake up."

"He's gone, isn't he? I need to let go, don't I? It's more than two years."

"I can't . . . I can't tell you what to do . . ."

"No. But you can kiss me. It's not too soon or too fast for that, is it, Brandon? Two years, three years. It's been a long time since this girl's been kissed and . . . and I'd like it to be a Marine who does it. Is that okay?"

"Does it matter to you if it's any Marine . . . I mean . . . I'm asking if any Marine will do?"

She smiled her small smile. "No, not any Marine will do, silly prince. I enjoyed the evening . . . the drive in, the meal, the movie, parking at this highway pullout and talking, the stars, your stories . . . your honesty . . . your courage . . . I've enjoyed it all. Now I want to enjoy this too. And I want you to be the Marine. Only you."

"Look. I was glad to do what I could for Ty. It wasn't enough, but I did what I could. Any Marine would have done it. You don't need to give me a thank you kiss. I'd . . . I'd rather wait for an 'I like you kiss' . . . if that's okay."

Her smile grew. "No, it's not okay. I want to be kissed now. Under the stars in your semi. I've been alone a long time. I know Ty's gone and I have to move on. You're the kindest thing that's happened to me since his smile. So please. I don't want you to give me everything. Just enough. Enough to bring me back to life again."

Brandon did not move.

She dropped her eyes and withdrew her hand from his arm. "I'm sorry. I thought there was a spark. There was for me. But I guess not for you. Let's just go. It's okay. My 'I like you" kiss is for another day. I know I'm not very pretty and . . ."

Brandon suddenly cupped her face in his large hands. "It really is a crazy world and you're the craziest woman in it if you think you don't cut it on looks. You're unreal you're so beautiful."

"Oh, Brandon, come on, I'm just a down home Pennsylvania girl who waits on tables and gets a few tips . . ."

The kiss did not last ten minutes, it did not even last five, but it lasted long enough for Kirsten Brittany MacLeod. She felt like she'd been starving, and now she had food, and drink, and the sort of passion from a man that was only a memory that brought pain, and tears, and sleepless nights. His arms went around her. She thought about the wounded arm, but both held her as tightly as rope and she couldn't tell one from the other – both were strong around her back, both drew her closer and closer to his chest, and to lips that might as well have been fire they put such heat in her face, and throat, and right down through her entire body. Her arms went around his neck, and she hung on for dear life as her mind exploded in bursts of light, and her skin turned to flames. Everything inside her shook and she clung to him more tightly to make it stop. When he broke away, she struggled to get her breath.

"Okay, okay," she murmured. "That was a wow. That was definitely a wow."

"Can't we . . . ?"

"No. No. I just want to keep this one in me. Maybe tomorrow. Maybe next week. But right now, this is it. This is all."

"All right."

"Don't be disappointed, please. You rocked my world more in three minutes than anything or anyone has done in two years. I want to see you again, Brandon. And again, and again, and again. But let me sit with this. Let me savor it. Your kiss meant everything to me. It's been such a long time of grieving. I've been stone inside. I've lost my life. Now I can feel the blood in my heart again. I have breath. Take me home, Marine. Take me home where I can relive your kiss with my pillow under my head. But take your time. Drive slow, Marine. Because I want to stare up at all the stars while we go.."

He smiled. "So, we really can get together again?"

She laughed. "Oh, yes. Absolutely, yes. Is that what you're worried about? That's the least of your worries, Marine."

"Yeah? And what's the worst?"

"I'll want your next kiss to be even better than this one. Spend your week on the road figuring that out."

He grinned. "Lol."

"Lol," she repeated and turned back to the window and the stars.

But Brandon had a longer spell to work on what might be a better kiss than he wanted. He had to make several long hauls to Calgary, Alberta and it was almost June before he texted Kirsten and asked her out again. By then, the kiss that had happened at the pullout near Philadelphia felt like a daydream, something he had imagined during his long hours on the road to make the time pass more quickly and pleasantly. What she was thinking he had no idea, but he was worried she'd tell him the kiss had been a mistake and that they needed to slow down. Or worse – that he needed to back off completely.

He'd always wondered why more men hadn't asked Kirsten out. He knew for some it had to do with Ty. They didn't want to date a woman who was so wrapped up in her dead fiancé she couldn't focus on anyone, but a ghost. Others found her too distant and hard to get to know, even though she came across friendly and upbeat at the diner. Away from serving tables and thanking men for generous tips, there weren't as many smiles or anywhere near as much laughter.

"It's like she's two different people," a friend had told him. "The Kirsten at the restaurant is one of them and everyone loves her. Then there's the Kirsten who can't forget her dead fiancé. And there's a third Kirsten, who's trying so hard to be Amish she might as well be dressed in black and driving a buggy."

"You really think that?" Brandon had responded.

"Just wait. You'll see. How many times have you gone out with her?"

"I don't know. Four or five."

"How much have the Amish come up?"

"A bit."

"One day she'll go Amish on you. Just wait."

Brandon made a face. "And what will *going Amish* look like?"

"Like someone forbidding you to clap even though every part of you is screaming to cheer for something you really like."

"And how do you know all this?"

"I went out with her twice about six months ago. I knew I was crazy to do it. But she's so good-looking and always has that big smile on her face at Zook's. But yeah, first date, all about Ty Samson, KIA, but still very much alive in Kirsten MacLeod's heart. Second date . . . Everything You Never Wanted To Know About The Amish And Were Afraid To Ask In Case Someone Told You. We didn't even get to the movie. That was it for me. Done."

Of course, she's going to be complicated, Brandon argued with himself. *How long has she been living on her own? Her father was KIA, her brother and her fiancé too, that's enough to twist anybody up inside. I just need to give her room to take in as much fresh air and space as she can.*

And hope, another voice told him, *that the kiss really meant something and still really means something.*

He hated himself for it, but he was so nervous before coming by her house he parked for half an hour two blocks away. *What are you? Sixteen and never been kissed?* But he stayed parked. Then he went to a shop that had tobacco, and whiskey, and flowers, and wanted to purchase a bouquet of roses. But half the roses had wilted. So, he bought six bouquets and moved the roses around until he had twelve that he liked.

"Huh." The sales clerk placed her hands on her hips. "I never saw a guy do anything like this. You must be desperate."

Brandon shrugged as he sorted through the roses. "A man's gotta do what a man's gotta do."

"Or maybe she's really worth it?"

"Oh, yeah. A definite on that. She really is worth it." Brandon held up the bouquet he'd created. "What do you think?"

"None of them are red," the sales clerk pointed out.

"I don't want red," he told her. "It's too soon for red."

She shrugged. Her name tag said Cyndy. "It's never too soon for red."

He shook his head. "Cyndy . . . it's for the woman I'm seeing tonight. We've dated . . . what . . . four times? It's not a red moment yet."

She shook her head back. "I'm sure you don't have it right. Look. I'm going to wrap up this red one. It's on the house. Keep it in your pickup. If she goes for the bouquet you've put together, and never mentions you've got every color but red, great, you're the local expert on Pennsylvania women. But if she laughs, and teases you, and wonders where the red rose is, tell her it's too special to give her with all of the others. Then whip out this one I'm giving you. Let her unwrap it. I bet you'll get a kiss."

Brandon shook his head. "I won't."

Cyndy smirked and shrugged with one shoulder. "Come back and tell me about it."

"All right. I will. *Adios*."

"Good luck." Brandon was wearing a black straw Stetson he'd picked up in Calgary. She flicked her eyes at his head and added, "Cowboy."

Which was the first word Kirsten used when she opened her front door and looked at him, "Cowboy!"

"Yeah . . . well . . . it's just a hat I picked up on the road . . ."

"I like it."

"You do?"

"Yeah. I do. Hey. I've missed you. I'm so glad you called."

"Yeah?"

"Yeah." Her smile was big. Bigger than he'd ever seen it. "Who are the roses for, Cowboy? Your girlfriend?"

"Uh . . . no . . . no . . . they're for you. A kinda spring thing." He thrust the bouquet at her as if they were burning a hole in his hand. "It's nice to see you again."

"Wow. They're beautiful." She put the roses to her nose and breathed in. "I love it. So, I'm not your girlfriend?"

"Well . . ."

"I'm just kidding. Let me put them in water and I'll be right back. Wait here."

He stood in the hall and looked at the pictures of her father and brother and Ty. He almost wondered if he would feel any condemnation from Ty, but the photograph was just a photograph. When she returned she was practically bouncing. She linked her arm through one of his and made him run to the pickup.

"Hey," he laughed. "What's the rush?"

"You're the rush," Kirsten responded, sliding into the truck. "I told you. I missed you. I've been counting the days. Haven't you?"

"I don't know about counting. But I think about you all the time. Is that okay?"

She grinned. "More than okay." When he got in behind the wheel she pressed her fingers into his arm. He was wearing a black T shirt so her fingers dug into his skin. "That kiss was something special. Did you forget all about it? Because I haven't."

"Believe me, Kirsten. I haven't."

"Yeah?"

"Yeah."

She laughed. "Yeah, yeah, yeah."

Her fingers were still on his arm, and the touch made his whole body feel warm, and his head a little light.

"Where are we going?" Kirsten asked.

She removed her fingers and his head cleared up.

"I thought we'd head over to Paradise and . . ."

She interrupted him. "There wasn't a red."

"What?"

51

"There were white roses, and pink, and yellow, and peach." She stared out the front windshield. "But not one red one. It was pretty obvious."

"And you think that means something? That I'm making a statement with that bouquet?"

"Aren't you? Why else give a girl flowers?"

"Look, Kirsten . . ."

"You don't have to explain. Let's just go. The roses you gave me are beautiful. I love them."

"Kirsten . . ."

"Really. I'm happy. I put on my fave top and jeans for you." He glanced down at her old jeans, and at her obviously faded, and obviously comfortable MADE IN MAUI T-shirt shirt, while she laughed. "Well worn. Life has polished my edges so I might as well wear stuff that reflects that."

"You look great."

"Thank you, kind sir."

"I wanted to say something else."

"No need. Let's get going, Cowboy. I'm starving."

"There's a thing in the back seat."

She looked at him and then twisted to look in the back of the crew cab. "A thing?"

"Wrapped up in green paper. It's for you."

"Really." She stretched out an arm and put it in her lap. "What now?"

"I don't know."

"You don't know?" She tore at the tissue paper with her fingers. In a moment, the red rose appeared. "Oh, my goodness. Oh, wow. You did this? For me? Why didn't you put it with the others?"

"A red rose is too special to put with the others. It kinda makes its own statement."

"Wow, we are all about statements tonight. The roses you bring, the outfit I'm wearing . . ." She put the red rose to her face. "Mmmm. Delicious. Hey. I guess you didn't forget about me, after all."

"What makes you think I did?"

Kirsten shrugged and continued to take in the scent of the rose. "It's been almost a month."

"I was hauling stuff north. I had a bunch of loads. I told you that."

"I know."

"But."

She shrugged. "I guess I wasn't sure. I guess I'm not sure about much these days. Oh, who am I kidding? I'm not sure about anything." She put her lips to the rose. "Except red roses maybe. I know what they mean. Or what they're supposed to mean."

Brandon took a risk. A huge risk. When he thought about it later, he stepped back and looked at himself as if he were a different creature. But at the moment, seeing Kirsten with the rose, listening to what she was saying and how she was saying it, he simply plunged. One moment he was gazing at her, the next he had taken her in his arms and covered her mouth with his. And everything inside him exploded.

She did not push him away. She curled into him and wrapped her arms around his back as if she were a vine. The kiss went on for a very long minute and he was surprised she never broke it off, but instead gripped him more and more tightly.

"I thought you were hungry," he murmured, but her lips quickly took away any other words he might say.

"I'm starving," she whispered. "But it's about a lot more than burgers and fries."

"Kirsten . . ."

"Hush. Hold me. Don't stop holding me. And prove to me that you care for me. Prove it every day in a hundred different ways."

Chapter 4

*K*irsten felt like she was in some kind of movie or book that had a happy ending on every page or after every scene. Nothing felt like a chore anymore and every weekend was Disneyland or better. Every weekend Brandon wasn't working, that is. When he was on the road, she lived for his texts and his phone calls late at night. Once he was home, she hoped every time the door swung open at the diner it would be him or that every knock at the door of her house would be his. Doing his chocolates and roses thing for her. But she didn't need more roses and she sure didn't need chocolates. Just him.

"You're all this girl wants," she'd tell him, lacing her arms about his neck. "You make my yesterdays look as if they're missing something, my todays like a coloring book, and all my tomorrows a sunrise over the Grand Canyon."

"Really." He laughed. "That sounds like what my old American Lit teacher Mrs. Pebble would call hyperbole."

"Don't use such big words. You're a Marine and a trucker. Marines and truckers don't use mouthfuls."

"Ones from the 21st century do."

"Oh, hyperbole away then. I don't care. I'm all hyperbole today. I've been nothing but hyperbole since our first kiss. I'm hyperbolic. Who cares? I love it!"

"Me too." He hugged her as hard as he dared without popping bones and crushing her lungs.

The dark cloud on Kirsten's Grand Canyon sunrise came the morning Joshua Miller walked back into the diner. She had her back turned to grab some salt and pepper shakers, glanced at the door as it opened, saw it was him, and turned her back to the door again and then slipped into the kitchen.

"Hey, where are you going?" demanded the cook. "It's crazy busy out there."

Kirsten went through the back door. "I'm on my smoke break, Sid."

"You don't smoke!"

There was a small table, and a few chairs for the staff up against the wall of the diner, and Kirsten took a chair in the shade. And began to fret. Which meant nail chewing came next. Not serious nail chewing. Just enough to keep one part of her occupied while the rest of her fretted. The last person in the world she ever wanted to see again was Joshua Miller.

"Excuse me?"

She looked up from her nails.

Joshua had come around the side of the diner.

"I know you are on your coffee break but . . ." he began.

From where she was sitting, he had a very unmanly, and very sheepish face on, and it irritated Kirsten far beyond biting her tongue. "What do you want?"

Her sharp tone made him hesitate. "You are not at the Schrocks as often as before."

"I'm there Monday to Thursday. That's good enough. My weekends are my own. I don't have to be a slave for the Yoder Amish."

Joshua's eyes were huge. "No one thinks of you . . . of you as a slave for . . . for the Yoder Amish."

Kirsten went back to her nails. "Of course, you do. I'm good enough to babysit the Amish, *ja?* But not good enough to be one of them."

"It is all a misunderstanding. I am sure at another meeting . . ."

"Oh, there's no misunderstanding at all. My father and my brother and my fiancé gave their lives so America could be safe and the Amish safe to worship as they wish within her borders. Yes, my family is good enough for that. Good enough to give their lives for your freedom of religion. But not good enough to be invited to become one of you."

"Kirsten . . ."

"Miss Macleod," she corrected him.

"Miss MacLeod . . ." he began again.

"Oh, just go away, Mr. Miller. I'm sorry to be rude but . . . but the four evenings I take care of the Schrocks' boy is enough for me. It's . . . it's enough Amish for me. Sure, there was a time I thought the Yoder Amish would be everything. But that's changed, Mr. Miller. Now there are things I want more. I'm really not that interested in the way . . . the way you people believe or do things . . . so if you can just wrap your head around that . . ."

Joshua took off his broad-brimmed black hat and started turning it in a circle in his hands. "It's important to me that I apologize. That is why I came here this morning. I know I insulted you . . . hurt you . . . the last time we were together. I was not thinking straight. I really wasn't. Your family, they have given all they had so we can be at peace. No, we Amish do not take up arms, but that doesn't mean we are supposed to be mean-spirited to those who differ from our ways. That is not how our Lord Jesus Christ would have us act towards those we disagree with and who do not embrace our faith. I am no fool, Miss MacLeod. There is a time for everything, a season for everything under heaven. In the past, our people were not safe in Europe. So, the Amish came to America. Here, for the most part, there has been protection from harm. Soldiers and police persecuted us in Europe, but in America they have become our defenders. Otherwise, who knows? It might have become another Europe for the Amish. So, your family has been part of that shield around us and around America. I understand this. Many of the Amish understand this. Forgive me for not honoring your family for what they have done for us . . . for everyone. I'm truly sorry."

As Joshua spoke, Kirsten took her fingers from her mouth and the hard lines around her eyes softened. When he had finished, she sat for a moment looking at the lane behind him and a chain link fence. Then she stood up and put out her hand. He took it.

"Thank you, Mr. Miller," she said and smiled. "Your apology and understanding mean a lot to me. I hope we can be friends again."

"Yes. I hope so too."

"Please come in and let me buy you a coffee. I'll have to get back to work."

"I wanted to ask . . . if you would like to bring Malachi to a shoeing . . . I am doing that Wednesday . . . I think he would like to see the horses . . . and hear the noise . . ." Joshua finally smiled for the first time. "The horses make plenty of noise on their own just by neighing, and stamping their hooves, and blowing, and shaking their manes . . . it would only be an hour . . . no more than an hour and a half . . . then you could share our dinner with us . . ."

"Hmm." Kirsten stood looking at him, thinking. "No to the dinner invitation, Mr. Miller. *Danke*. But no. Though it's a kind gesture. However, the shoeing? Malachi would love that. Wednesday?"

"At five. I will come by and . . ."

Kirsten shook her head. "We can take care of ourselves. Malachi and I will be there at five sharp. It's a kind invitation. Thank you again. Now do you want that coffee?"

Joshua grinned. "*Ja*. I'd like that very much."

So, he sat at the counter between a farmhand, and a sheriff's deputy, and it was a little like old times. She spoke with him as she hurried back and forth and once they both laughed together. But just like with her old vision of joining the Amish faith, things had changed. There was no spark with Joshua anymore. He was an interesting customer at the diner, dressed in black, with a long lanky body and a slim tanned face and blue eyes. Yes, he was handsome. But that was all.

"I'll see you on Wednesday," she promised when he got up to leave, and then rushed back into the kitchen to tell the cook about a special vegan breakfast he needed to prepare for a customer. When she returned, she didn't realize Joshua was gone for about five minutes. It made her shake her head. "You really have done a number on me, Brandon Peters. It seems I don't even notice old flames anymore. Not that he was ever a flame, I guess. But now Josh Miller's not even an ember."

Malachi laughed and swung from side-to-side in his wheelchair while Joshua hammered at horseshoes that Wednesday evening. The boy was fascinated by the flames of the forge, the sparks swirling upwards, how Joshua crouched, and held a horse's leg under his arm, and tapped a shoe into place on the hoof, how the horses stood and turned their heads to look at Malachi as happiness burst out of him. Kirsten liked watching Joshua's skill, at how good he was with the horses and the tools, and yes, she had to admit, she enjoyed watching the firelight flicker over his dark, handsome features, at the beads of sweat forming on his brow and trickling slowly along his face, at the flames bright in his deep blue eyes, at the strength in his arms and chest. Even though he wore a sleeveless top underneath the work shirt, his youth and perfection were obvious to her and she forced herself to look away several times.

A beautiful healthy Amish man, Kirsten thought to herself, *and I could have him all to myself with a nod of my head and the right sentence out of my mouth. But really, I don't want complicated. Brandon is wonderful. I don't need more wonderful.*

Still. She wondered what it would be like to kiss an Amish man. Almost wished Joshua would look at her – he would not look at her at all – put down his tools, wipe his hands and face on a towel, approach her while Malachi was fixated on the horses, lead her off to the side, take her in his so obviously strong arms, and kiss her. She didn't care if his shirt smelled of horses and hot steel, didn't care if there was sweat, didn't care if his hair was full of smoke, she just wanted a moment of that Amish kindness, and gentleness, and strength to wrap her up and take her away.

What would it feel like to be caught up in his arms and feel totally safe and secure? What would his lips be like compared to Brandon's? How hard would he kiss her, how long, how deep? His looks were so dark, and fiery, and appealing her head began to spin along with her imagination. It was like being attracted to a man from another country, and a different culture, and being overwhelmed by his unique mannerisms, and language, and charm. The Amish were American, but different American.

For several long minutes in Joshua's blacksmith shop, ridiculous fantasies about being held and kissed by Joshua – she tossed them off as ridiculous, but could not stop herself from indulging in them – whirled through Kirsten's mind, and she didn't know why they had suddenly erupted into her thoughts on this visit and never before. He was tender. Sensitive. Strong. Sweet. Caring. And absolutely overwhelming when it came to being a man. She shook her head several times, as if sparks had caught in her long hair, while her daydreams engulfed her.

You are being such a stupid and silly young woman, she snapped at herself. *What on earth has gotten into you? You have a boyfriend, for heaven's sake. And he's an amazing boyfriend and just as much a man as Joshua Miller. Basically – share it with all of us so we can come to some understanding of your crazy idiosyncrasies – what is your problem, Kirsten Brittany MacLeod? No . . . take us further . . .*

please . . . what are your deep-rooted and deep-seated problems that have you in a sixteen- year-old girl's headspace, while an Amish man shoes horses in front of you? I mean, really? Can you explain yourself in a way any of us listening in are able to understand at all?

As she watched - her eyes on Malachi, and Joshua, and the chestnut mare Joshua was shoeing - her mind continued to spin scenarios of Josh falling hopelessly in love with her. Suddenly, he shrugged first one suspender strap off his shoulder, and then the other, so that they dangled down around his knees while he worked. For whatever reason, this totally fascinated her, and in her wildly spinning imagination, she knew it would feel wonderful to be held against his chest by his arms . . . arms that were free of the bind of the suspenders.

"They bite into your shoulders when you are working hard," Joshua explained without looking up from his shoeing. "It's very uncomfortable."

Kirsten nodded. "I can only imagine."

He invited her and Malachi to dinner again. She said no. He invited her and Malachi back the next week when he would be shoeing some work horses, huge Percherons. She said no, yes, no, yes. No, no, no. And found herself there with Malachi five days later while Joshua grinned up at them, and lifted the enormous muscular legs of matched gray Percherons under his arm, and nailed large horseshoes into place.

Kirsten had sworn to herself she would not talk. She began to talk. "That must be so difficult,

Mr. Miller . . . Joshua . . . Josh . . . those legs must be so heavy."

"It is not so bad, Miss MacLeod."

"What if they kick you? I mean, wouldn't that be it for you? Wham?"

"Oh, ha ha, really, they are gentle giants." He patted the flank of the gray Percheron he was working on. "Cynthia would never hurt me, Miss MacLeod. Would you, girl?"

"Kirsten," she said.

"*Vas?*" he responded.

"I'm Kirsten."

He glanced up at her, the sweat making his face shine. "*Ja.* Of course, you are."

Kirsten had sworn to herself she would not daydream about the two of them being a couple. She began to daydream. At home, it had been easier to thrust her romantic thoughts about Josh from her mind. In his shop, she could not. She imagined Malachi falling asleep in his chair. Josh noticing this after he had finished with a Percheron. Leading the large horse outside and tethering it. Returning. Splashing cold water over his face and arms. Using a ladle to take a drink from a basin. Smiling at her. Coming towards her. Smoothing down her hair with his large gentle hands. Putting his arms around her waist. Pulling her against him. Placing his lips against her hair, her forehead, her eyes. Her mouth was on fire waiting for him to stop there. When he finally did she sighed like a summer wind and put all her strength and heat into her kisses. She knew he liked them.

"My gentle giant," she purred.

She smelled like June weather, sunshine and showers, but Josh smelled of Percherons, and nails, and fire, and sweat, and she didn't care. She liked it. He kissed her so tenderly. Kisses, kisses, and more kisses, kisses all afternoon, while Malachi napped. Then he lay down on a patch of clean straw and fell asleep. And it was the most wonderful feeling in the world to stand there and watch over him. The young woman protecting and shielding her mighty warrior. Her mind – as wild as crazy as it had been – got even crazier and took them to MacLeod lands in Scotland, and to the grassy slope of a sun-soaked hill, with the color of wildflowers all around them. He was in a kilt, and she in a skirt, and a great sword was strapped to his back, and his hands were just as large, and just as gentle as they had been in Pennsylvania, and he held her against the shirt he was wearing, the same way he held her against his work shirt as they embraced by the forge in his blacksmith shop.

"You're Scottish," she whispered.

"I'm whatever you want me to be," he answered.

"I love Scotland."

"I love you."

"That's sweet," she murmured. "Thank you. I've wanted to hear that for so long."

"All right. I have to ask. Will you stay to dinner?"

Kirsten blinked. "What?"

"Every visit my mother insists I ask."

Kirsten gave her head a short shake to clear it. "To dinner. Yes. How sweet of her. Poor thing. She never gets a yes. Well, next time you will get a yes."

"Next time?"

"Next time. If you invite us back to the smithy you will get a yes."

Josh grinned. "Wonderful. Wow . . . as you *Englisch* say."

She laughed. "Yes. It is a wow. Believe me. It really is."

At home, she could not sleep.

"I don't want to be Amish anymore," she said to God and the ceiling. "I don't, I don't, I don't."

She turned on her side. "Regardless of my silly schoolgirl thoughts about Josh, I don't want anything more to do with the Yoder Amish. Amen."

She flipped over on her other side. "Brandon will save me. He will make me laugh, he will kiss me, he will tell me how pretty I am, and my whole world will be right side up again. Wait and see. He's back from his road trip tomorrow. Just wait and see."

But once Brandon returned from his road trip, he made everything worse.

Chapter 5

*T*here had been ice cream cones. There had been ice cream popped onto her nose. There had been squeals of laughter – hers – and shouts of laughter – his. They had wrestled on the grass. More ice cream on more noses. And chins. And cheeks. Children playing on swings, and slides, pointed at them and laughed too.

"Those kids are so cute." Kirsten sat up, brushing grass from her jeans.

"They are." Brandon sat up beside her. "Not as cute as you, but they're pretty cute."

"Yeah, yeah." She hugged her knees to her chest and leaned her head against his shoulder. "I want five million of them."

"Ha."

"No. Really. I do."

"Five million of them?"

"Well. Five then. Five kids full of spit and vinegar."

Brandon groaned. "What a nightmare that would be."

"Why?"

"Five kids messing up your day. Five kids messing up your life. You can't do this. You can't go there. All your money disappearing into their diapers, and clothes, and baby food. And then they're teenagers and it's even worse. No, thanks."

"You're kidding. Right?"

"I'm not kidding."

She took her head off his shoulder and looked at him. "You don't want kids? Not even one kid?"

"Not even one kid."

"Wow."

"So that makes me a bad person?"

"No. It's just . . ."

"What?"

"It doesn't make you at all like me."

Brandon shrugged. "I didn't know I had to be exactly like you."

"You don't. But on certain things we have to have common ground. When it comes to raising a family . . ."

"Whoa. Raising a family? All of a sudden we're married and raising a family?"

"So, you never think about it?"

"Marrying you? Okay, sure. But kids? No. They're not in my picture of a perfect marriage and a happy home."

"Why not?"

"They're just not. If I'm going to be married to you I just want to be married to you. Not to them. Not to a bunch of kids. Just you and me. That's enough."

"Well, it's not enough for me. I want a family. And that's more than two. It's at least three."

"And three is too much for me, Kristen MacLeod."

"And two isn't nearly enough for me, Brandon Peters."

"Fine."

"Fine."

After that there was no more ice cream on the nose, no more park, no more anything. Kirsten begged off the rest of the date, claiming a migraine, and Brandon drove away to meet up with his buddies. They didn't speak to each other for a couple of days and then he was on the road again. And this time he didn't text and he didn't call.

Kirsten was cross at work, cross at home, cross at God, pretty much cross at everyone and anything. Except Malachi. When she saw him he softened her heart. And Josh. She wanted to be cross at him. She had decided it was his fault that Brandon and her weren't on speaking terms. But the magic she swore to herself she didn't want always appeared – *poof!* – and she found herself admiring him and daydreaming while he worked. Even his family had a magical effect on her now. The last meal had been uncomfortable. This one was like easing into a pair of lightweight moccasins, it felt so good.

His parents were polite. His siblings made her smile, especially Rebecca, ten, who was always asking her cheerful questions and fetching her glasses of lemonade or sweet tea. Nothing came up about war or soldiers or Kirsten's rejection by the bishop and pastors. By the end of the evening, she regretted she had driven Malachi and herself to the house because it would have been much nicer to enjoy a buggy ride home under the June stars.

"I hope you will come again." Josh walked her to her truck, wheeling Malachi in his chair. "Many more times."

"Thank you, Josh. I'm sure I will. I enjoyed myself this evening."

"*Ja?*"

She laughed. "*Ja.*"

He grinned. "Good. Very good."

She laughed again. "Don't you mean *gut, das ist gut?*"

He laughed too. "*Ja*, that is what I mean."

After he had strapped Malachi into his seat, and folded up the chair and placed it in the bed of the pickup, Kirsten held out her hand. He took it. She gave him a gentle squeeze and he responded with a squeeze of his own. She giggled. Then she was in her truck and driving Malachi home. But in her mind both of them were in a buggy, and Josh was holding the reins just right, and the driver – what the Amish called the horse that pulled them – was trotting just right, and the June stars, well, in her mind they were just right too.

"You are insane," she told the mirror while she was brushing her teeth. "Brandon is perfect. And Josh? Okay, well, maybe Josh is perfect too. But in a different way. And not your way."

"Of course, it's my way."

She glared at the mirror, brushing ferociously, as if she could change her life with a toothbrush. "It is not."

"Is. He's good-looking, he's strong, he's gentle, he's smart . . ."

"So is Brandon. He's crazy good-looking."

"And Josh is a family man. Wants kids. Adores his siblings. You see how he takes care of them."

"Shut up."

"A strong, hot, good-looking family man with a solid work ethic and a solid faith."

"I told you to shut up. I can brush my teeth without a mirror, you know."

"Brandon falls short, sister."

"He does not."

"He falls way short of your desires and your dreams."

Kirsten spat into the sink, rinsed out her mouth, and spat again. "I'm leaving now."

"Betcha can't leave Josh lol."

"Betcha I can. Lol yourself."

But try as Kirsten might to place Brandon in her "just before sleep" dreams, he was still on the road, he still hadn't texted or called, and she was still angry with him. So, Joshua had no problem intruding. He wiped his arm across his forehead, sipped water from the ladle, smiled at her, approached her - face popping with sweat from the forge, blue eyes like a knife to her heart - and began a long, slow kiss that reminded her of a burning wick. Her knees practically buckled. His arms held her up. As the long kiss continued, she curled one of her legs around his, a leg complete with blue jeans, rhinestones, and cowgirl boots. He kind of melted into her arms.

Wow, that was a rush . . . the big, tall, strong Amish blacksmith and farrier, melting under her kisses. She kept it up until her imagination was more real to her than the bed she was lying on or the roof over her head, and Josh was so in love with her he didn't want anyone or anything else. *Even if I must leave the Amish faith, I will do it,* he swore to her between kisses, *because you mean more to me than the church. God understands. He is everywhere. You do not need to be Amish to know God. Just be who you are, where you are. For God is love.*

"And do you love me?" she asked in a quiet voice. "Do you truly love me, Joshua Miller?"

"You know I do. You know it."

"*Ja.*" She smiled in the dark of her room. "I do know it."

Two days later Brandon showed up at her door at nine at night with a bouquet of roses. This time they were all red. Even under the porch light, Kristen could see they were as red as blood. As red as hearts.

"I'm sorry," he said, before she could open her mouth. "It's all my fault. I say I don't want kids and yet I'm acting like the worst kid on the block."

"Brandon . . ."

"Okay so I don't want kids. But I want you. I hope that's enough."

"I have . . ."

"Let's just make up. Kiss and make up. I've been an idiot. I'm so sorry."

"Let's sit down on the porch swing and talk."

"I just don't want anyone or anything to come between us. That would drive me wild. Nothing's going on, is there?"

"Hush."

"I would go crazy. Out of my head. All my fault. That Amish guy . . . does that Amish guy mean anything to you? I know you were sweet on him a few months back . . ."

"Shh. There is nothing going on. I take Malachi to watch him blacksmith, that's all. Now and then I have a meal with the Miller family. Nothing is going on with Joshua. Nothing."

"Because I would go crazy, Kirsten."

"There is nothing to go crazy about."

"You're my girl."

"Yes, I'm for sure your girl."

"I just want us to make up. I just want things to be right between us."

"Well, the roses are going to go a long way to getting us back in the same headspace and the same heart space. A few hugs would help too."

He took her in his arms on the porch swing. "And kisses?"

"For sure kisses. I need lots of kisses."

And she did. She knew she did. The imaginary ones with Josh were killing her. They weren't real, they weren't true, and she didn't love him and had no intention of ever loving him. She wanted real world. And she was confident

Brandon could give that back to her and stop her head from spinning in wild circles around Joshua Miller's smithy.

But his first kiss didn't do anything for her. It was fast and clumsy and rough. His second kiss was just as bad. Kirsten began to panic. Her handsome Marine was supposed to be her salvation.

"Slow down," she whispered in his ear. "Take your time. You don't have to fix us in ten seconds. Give us an hour. Give us two. Make it three. And we'll be all right."

And they were. When he finally went home and she was in bed, with the roses in water on a table beside her, all her thoughts were about Brandon, and the days ahead, and even a lifetime ahead. She did not think about the forge, or Josh Miller, or the children she had already picked out names for. When her and Malachi went out to see Joshua work on more Percherons – using her truck, she wouldn't dream of asking Joshua to pick them up in the buggy now – all she saw was the hard work, and the horseshoes, and Malachi's delight with everything. If a blue-eyed, strong-armed Josh Miller daydream floated her way, she just pushed it aside and let Brandon fill the vacuum. Which he did admirably with his wonderful physique, and wonderful kisses, and wonderful words.

"It's so good to have you back," she told him.

"No more of those long hauls for at least a month. Not until late July."

"Good. So good."

"We can BBQ, have some friends over, swing on that swing of yours . . . Hey, we can take some day trips. How about Gettysburg? Have you ever been?"

"No." she smiled at his enthusiasm. "I've never been to Gettysburg."

"Would you like that? Would you like to take a trip out there? It's awesome."

"Yes, I'd like that very much, Brandon. So long as you promise me our side wins."

He laughed. "For sure our side will win. You and I will always win."

"Then let's not waste any more time. Let's go."

And Gettysburg was beautiful even though it was a battle site. She forgot about everything . . . Lancaster, Lancaster County, Zook's Diner, Bishop Yoder, skinny as a hoe handle Pastor Gore and, most important of all, Josh Miller and his knife-cut blue eyes. Brandon and her followed a guide most of the day, then broke off and relaxed in a grove of ancient trees in which hundreds of Minie balls were embedded. After that, they had a meal in the town. They did most of their talking over coffee. Lying in her bed hours later, Kirsten could hardly remember what they had discussed. But his kisses she didn't forget. She went over every one of them. And smiled before falling asleep. Suddenly it wasn't about the dream kisses of Josh Miller anymore. Just the real ones of Brandon Peters.

Chapter 6

June
Thursday night, the Schrocks, 8:35 PM

*W*e asked that you stay behind after Malachi was asleep so that we could have a chat," said Lydia Schrock. "Would you like some tea?"

Hair up in a tight bun, Kirsten sat with her hands in the lap of her long black dress. "All right."

Lydia poured. "Cream, dear?"

"A bit. *Danke*."

Adam Schrock stretched out his long legs as he sat across from Kirsten in his favorite armchair. "All is well with you?"

"It is, Adam. Thank you for asking."

"You still enjoy caring for our boy?"

"Of course. My goodness, Adam, what a question."

"You find no fault with Mrs. Schrock or I?"

Lydia sat down beside Kirsten on the couch.

Kirsten gave her a puzzled look.

Then narrowed her eyes at Adam. "Why are you saying these things to me?"

He lifted both his hands, palm upwards. "I am wondering . . . we are both wondering . . ."

He paused.

Kirsten waited. But she felt like biting her nails.

Adam sighed and sat forward, facing her. "It used to be you wished nothing more than to be one of us. To dress as we dress, worship as we worship, marry as we marry, and raise families to the glory of the Lord. Every time you came to our house to care for our son, you wanted to know something more about our faith. You could not wait to be baptized. And now, it is almost as if we do not exist."

"Do not exist?" Kirsten was taken aback. "How can you say I act like that when I am with your son four days of the week?"

Adam shrugged while Lydia looked on, hands knotted in her lap.

"All right then." Now Kirsten leaned forward. "Let us be honest with one another. Yes, my ardor has cooled when it comes to the Amish faith. But why has it cooled? Was it my desire that I become less of an enthusiast for the Amish way? No. It was you people who turned your back on me. It was you who told me to go away. It was you who declared I was not worthy. So, is it any wonder I have stopped knocking at the door of the Yoder Amish? One of your ministers said there was no place for me among you even if I were baptized one hundred times. That is pretty final, don't you think? And, if I may say so, extremely hurtful and insulting."

Lydia spoke up. "We did not turn our backs on you. God forbid."

"But your bishop did. And you obey your bishop, don't you?"

"*Ja,* of course we do."

"So, I am good enough to help you both out and care for Malachi. But I am not good enough to be Amish. Is that how it works?"

"Of course not. Kirsten, my dear, what has gotten into you?"

Kirsten felt the anger rising in her, and one part of her mind told it to stop, but another said to go ahead, Adam and Lydia needed to hear what she had to say with some vinegar in it, and that was the part of her that won out.

"What has gotten into me?" blurted Kirsten. "When have I been anything but faithful? When have I ever let you down? I love Malachi. I love you. But the Amish people do not return that love."

Adam and Lydia both responded at the same time using the same words: "Of course, we return that love."

"By rejecting me?"

"We are bound to honor and obey our bishop," Adam replied. "But we have our own feelings about the matter. If it were up to us, you would be baptized Amish tomorrow."

"You cannot change his mind, can you?" Kirsten challenged them. "Not his or Pastor Gore's, not any of them. They have absolute power over you."

Adam's face hardened. "Not absolute. God alone has absolute power over me. Over Lydia. Over any of the Amish men or women."

"Then disagree."

"What are you saying?" Adam demanded.

"Disagree. If you feel the bishop and pastors are wrong, disagree with them. God has absolute power over you, not them. So, disagree."

"It is not so simple."

"Of course, it's simple. It's as simple and straightforward as one of your plow furrows. God directs your steps. Not man. God Almighty, yes? So, does God tell you to reject me?"

"No. Never."

"Tell your bishop that. Tell him God favors me. Tell him God wants to include me in the Amish church. Tell him that is what you also believe."

Adam shook his head. "I . . . I cannot. We cannot."

"Why not? God is the one you answer to."

"*Ja*, but he puts men of his choosing in authority over us. We are bound to obey."

"As if they were God?"

"Not as if they were God." Adam searched for the words. "But as if God was speaking to us and directing us through them."

Lydia nodded in agreement with her husband.

"So . . . you are saying . . ." Kirsten also searched for her words. "God spoke through them to me."

Adam did not respond.

"That when I was told I would not be fit for the Yoder Amish if I were baptized a hundred times over, that was God?"

"Those were the words they chose to employ," Lydia replied. "It does not mean those were God's words, his exact words."

"But . . . the intent would be the same," Kirsten said.

Adam shook his head. "My dear. Please. This is not a court of law."

"God might have said it differently. But it amounts to the same thing, doesn't it? When your bishop and pastors were saying no to me, they were being directed by God to say that. If you say that is not so, that the bishop was not necessarily hearing the voice of God correctly in this instance, then God is not rejecting me, and you ought to stand up, and tell your bishop to baptize me."

"My dear, my dear . . ."

Kirsten sat up straight. "Oh, yes, I know. It is not that simple. But, I suppose, for me, it is that simple. Either God is speaking through your bishop and denying me baptism into the Amish faith or he is not. If you think God is not denying me baptism, you should speak up. But you will not. Because you really do believe God is speaking through your bishop and pastors."

She got to her feet. "I am not wanted, am I? And those who do want me will not fight for me. I have loved the Amish faith for years. And I have loved serving your family for just as long. But now we must part ways. I have a young man who truly loves me and who *does* stand up for me. We will get married one day, very soon, and start a new life together. God will be part of that life. But not your God. There are many churches in this county. The God of those churches shall be our God."

Adam and Lydia rose. Their faces winced as if both had been struck physical blows.

"What are you saying?" asked Adam.

Kirsten unbound her hair and it fell past her shoulders. "That I am moving on. That you and the Yoder Amish were once a huge part of my life, but now they are not. You have said I do not belong among you and now I realize that is true – I don't. I love Malachi so much. So, if you wish I will continue to be his caregiver. I cannot just walk off and leave that dear heart." Tears came into one of her eyes. "And he is such a dear heart. If only your bishop and pastors were was like him."

"Kirsten, my dear." Lydia reached out to her. "We should pray."

"No. We should go."

She left the house, got into her truck and drove away. Adam and Lydia were at the door, but she did not have it in her to wave. Tears were streaking down her face and she had to keep swiping at her eyes with the back of her hand so that she could see. It felt to her as if she had been driving for hours by the time she arrived at her house. A car was sitting on the street she did not recognize. But she recognized the uniforms of the men who got out of it and who approached her, almost in step, once she had parked her truck.

They were Marines.

Chapter 7

*K*irsten sat at her bedroom window waiting for the sun to come up. It would still be a couple of hours. She didn't mind. The dark was fine with her. If the entire day remained dark it might be a good thing. Like the black dress she was wearing.

His remains had been found by a patrol in a remote area of the desert. The wreck of the chopper he'd been in was more than a mile north of the body. Some of his bones had been scattered by wild animals. But his dog tags were still intact. And the dental records had confirmed his identity beyond a shadow of a doubt. Sergeant Ty Samson, USMC, was coming home.

He would be buried next to her father and mother and brother, as if he were family. Because to her, Ty was family. Years had gone by since he'd been listed as MIA and she had come to accept he was probably dead. But the shock of the two Marines telling her that, that the prayers at the back of her mind were over, that any lingering half-hope no longer existed, made her sink to her knees in the doorway. She knew the Marines who had been sent to her had been trained not to touch grieving parents or wives or family, no matter how hard they took the news of the loss of a loved one. But both Marines reached down to help to her feet and both walked her to a couch in the living room. They asked if the Corps could call someone and both made her tea before leaving. They probably shouldn't have saluted her. But they did.

The mayor had come to her personally to ask if there could be a   funeral procession. He wanted schools involved, the scouts, the police, and the fire departments. To him, it was important that citizens remembered men and women were still giving their lives for America's freedom. She was numb, her mind blank, and she just nodded. He took her hand. She smiled as tears made their way down her face. Ty liked marches, and parades, and he cleaned up well in his dress blues, so why not?

She could not understand was the intensity of her pain or her desire to close and lock the door of her house and retreat to the den. For a long time, Ty had only been a memory. She had begun dating again, for heaven's sakes. Yet the Marines at her door had rocked her world in the worst of ways. Brandon called a hundred times, but she wouldn't pick up her iPhone. Finally, he'd simply come through a window in the basement, and walked upstairs, and found her in the den. Once she saw him she burst into fresh tears. But she would not go to him.

"I'm sorry, so sorry, Brandon," she sobbed. "I don't know what's wrong with me. It's not like he was just killed yesterday or something."

"It's okay. It's totally okay."

"You've been so kind. I really trust you. But I can't let another man hold me right now. I can't."

"I get it. I do. It doesn't matter how long ago his chopper went down and he went missing, Kirsten. You got the news he was KIA a couple of days ago and that's when died for you. Not before."

"Thank you. Yes. That's it. Thank you."

"I . . . I just want to say how sorry I am. Sorry for his death. Sorry for your pain. I'm glad the town is going to go all out for him."

"It . . . it seems a bit much . . ."

Brandon shook his head. "It isn't. Every town and city in the USA ought to be doing this kind of welcome . . . no matter how any of us come home from the wars."

"I don't know how I'll get through that day. I honestly don't."

"You're strong, Kirsten, really strong. You'll do Ty and all of us proud."

"Are you . . . will you . . .?"

Brandon looked away. "I'm on the road. South and west this time. California and Nevada."

"What? You mean . . ."

"I can't make it to the processional. I can't be there. I'm sorry."

"Can't you ask them . . .?"

"No. They'll just give the job to someone else. I need this one. I need the money." He shrugged, but still wouldn't look at her. "Besides. You're standing there and I'm standing here. What can I do? You don't need me. You need Ty. I can't do anything for you right now."

Her eyes widened in surprise. "Of course, I need you, Brandon. I need you more than ever. Just because . . . I can't be held . . . it doesn't mean I don't need your support. It's really important to me that you be there."

"I don't think so. You need your space. You're grieving. What do you want with a boyfriend when your fiancé just died? After I'm back from the coast, it'll be easier for us to talk."

"I'm not going to feel okay in a snap of your fingers, Brandon. It'll take a few weeks. Or months. I need you. I need to be able to talk to you."

He finally made eye contact and gave her a crooked smile. "We will. Once the funeral is over. Once he's interred. Once I'm back from LA. We'll talk forever then. We'll get everything sorted out."

"Right now is when I'm sorting stuff out in my head and heart, Brandon. That's when I need you the most. Right now."

"Our time will come, Kirsten, it will. Look. Don't you have others who can be with you? Good friends?"

"No."

"Sure, you do. What about that Amish family you work for? You take care of their kid four or five nights a week, right? They'll stand with you."

"Oh, I hardly speak with them anymore, Brandon. It's just me and their son really. No, they won't stand with me, Brandon. They can't. They're pacifists. Conscientious objectors. They're against all forms of warfare and bloodshed. You know that."

"Hey. No one's asking them to fight in Afghanistan or Syria or something. Just be with a young woman who's lost a person important to her. How does that support the war effort? How does that kill anybody?"

"If they stand beside me at the procession, it will look like they condone warfare, and killing, and they're not going to do that. They'll pray for me. They'll be kind to me. Despite our differences, they've already expressed their condolences. But they won't stand with me and all the other citizens who will be saluting or waving the Stars and Stripes or placing their hands over their hearts. They will never do something like that. Never."

"It's a funeral. Not a call to arms."

"They will not honor the war dead because they do not believe in war. Ty Samson should not have enlisted in an organization designed solely for the purpose of killing other human beings. That is how they see it. That is the only way they see it. They cannot be persuaded otherwise." She made a chopping motion with her hand. "Done."

"Is that what their God thinks?'

Kirsten shook her head and curled into a large leather armchair. "I don't know what their God thinks."

"You don't? After spending all that time with them? Eating in their homes? Trying to join their church? You don't know what their God thinks?"

"I know what they think. I know what I think. And that's all I know."

"Well, I can take a shot at it. *Greater love has no man than this than that a man lay down his life for his friends.* That's from the Bible. I heard it read a hundred times over there. The chaplains used it all the time. And you know what? That's what God thinks."

He turned to go. "Look. I'll call you as soon as I get back. Until then, I'm not going to bother you. I'm not going to intrude. You need your space. I'm there for you. In spirit, you know? But when you're ready, I'll be right at your side, Kirsten."

"I'm ready now," she replied quietly, looking down at her hands.

"No. You're not."

So, Kirsten took up the mayor's offer of traveling in an open car with him and his wife during the procession. It was better than sitting in a vehicle by herself. Sure, staff at the diner would have sat with her if she'd asked. But she didn't ask. She didn't ask anyone to do anything. Flowers, and cards, and meals found their way to her home just the same. Including Amish meals.

The Yoder Amish. Who she knew would not and could not be on Main Street when they brought Ty home. She did not look for them. Her staff at the diner, yes, she expected to see them, and she did, in a group with their spouses and children, standing resolute, hands on hearts, hats off, saluting, the children waving flags as the motorcade moved slowly through the town and out to the cemetery. She expected to see her customers from the diner as well, and she did, scattered throughout the crowds lining the sidewalks and streets. Friends of her family, people who had known her since she was young, known her parents, known her brother, known Ty, they were all there along with students from the elementary, the middle schools, and the high schools. The state police, and local police, and the sheriff's deputies stood in ranks by their cruisers and saluted. The firefighters and EMTs stood by their waxed and polished trucks. Staff from her home care service were there. They were all there.

As the line of vehicles moved along, Ty just ahead of her in the hearse where the flag-draped coffin was clearly visible, she found she could not stop crying, and the tears blurred her vision so that it was impossible to make out all the faces of the men, and women, and children that stood for her and the man who would have been her husband. She was almost angry with herself. Why was she still crying so hard when she'd been dealing with her grief for not only days but years? The mayor's wife, Clarissa, was next to her, and took her hand, and squeezed it.

All right, Ty, she said to herself. *All right, God. All right, Pennsylvania. I am going to make it through this.*

A huge banner was spread over the street by the park. It had Ty's name on it, and his rank, and his Marine division, along with the date of his birth and the date of his death. WELCOME HOME, it read, TO ONE OF OUR OWN. A knife seemed to cut into her heart and the tears slipped down her cheeks all over again. Clarissa gave her a Kleenex. Then she placed the whole box in Kirsten's lap and took her hand again.

Once they were past the banner, Kirsten fought to pull herself together. The crowds were beginning to thin out. They were close to the edge of town. In a little while, they would pull into the cemetery. There would be an honor guard there. The firing of a military salute. They would fold the flag in a very precise way and hand it to her personally. She had to be ready for all of that. She had to be strong.

I will be, Ty, she whispered. *I will be.*

And then

They were there.

Impossible.

But no.

They were there.

Tall. Straight. Dark. Unmoving. Hands at their sides.

The Amish.

Not all of them.

Not the bishop.

Not the pastors.

But the Schrocks stood on the sidewalk with Malachi in his chair.

The Millers were there in one long row, the mother and father, the eight younger children, and at the end of the line, Joshua.

There were some others that she barely knew, but their clothing was distinctive. They were Amish, Yoder Amish.

They stood as straight as oaks and did not waver.

When Ty's coffin reached them, the men removed their large broad-brimmed black hats, and bowed their heads.

She saw Joshua's lips moving. He appeared to be praying.

Many lips were moving. Many prayers were being said.

For her. She knew that.

But also for Ty.

Prayers were being said for the soul of Ty Samson, USMC.

She thought the sight of Amish men and women attending a Marine's funeral procession would open the floodgates even more. Instead, Kirsten found it had a calming effect on her. The Amish faith in God, and in the ultimate goodness of life, put her in a different headspace and heart space. Her tears dried up and, when the motorcade turned through the gates of the cemetery, she even felt a measure of peace. This held through the entire graveyard cemetery, through the sharp and sudden firing of three volleys by Marines in dress blues, and it was still there when a Marine handed her the flag from Ty's coffin, carefully and precisely folded, placing it gently in her hands.

"I am sorry for your loss, ma'am," he said. "Thank you for his service to our country."

"God bless you." She had been able to smile. "God bless America."

"God bless America," he had responded.

The whole time at the cemetery Kirsten kept glancing at the open gates at the entrance. Three buggies and their horses were there, just outside the graveyard, and the Amish stood beside them, as sharp, and black, and still as silhouettes. They did not flinch as the rifles fired in a final salute and they did not look away when she was handed Ty's flag. But once the ceremony was finished, she looked, and they were gone.

Despite the protests of the diner's managers, Kirsten was back at work the next day, a very busy summer Saturday, and on Monday evening she was at the Schrocks.

"Thank you for being at the procession on Friday," she told them as she prepared Malachi for a trip out of doors. "I was caught off guard. I . . . didn't think you would do something like that."

"Why not?" responded Lydia.

"The flags . . . the patriotism . . . the military uniforms . . . the Marines . . . a man killed fighting a war . . ."

"We were not there for the Marines or the flags or the uniforms. We were there for God. We were there for the human heart."

"And the bishop does not mind?"

"Oh, he minds very much. We were reprimanded publicly this last Sunday meeting." Lydia hesitated, but decided to tell Kirsten more. "Joshua was singled out."

Kirsten snapped her head up from settling Malachi comfortably in his chair. "What? Why?"

Adam shrugged. "We don't know. He accepted the rebuke with an easy grace."

"Is this going to become an issue?" Kirsten looked from Adam's face to Lydia's. "I don't want that. Ty wouldn't have wanted that. Go ahead and say you're sorry if that makes life easier for you. It doesn't matter to me what you tell them. What matters is that you were there on Friday. That's what counts. And I'll never forget it."

"None of us will be permitted to take part in Communion at the end of August. The Yoder Amish only do it three times a year and we regret that we cannot break bread with our brothers and sisters before the Lord. We shall not be permitted to take part in the foot-washing either." Adam smiled. "So, we all have journeys with God Almighty. The Amish journey is different, but it is a journey nevertheless. There too we find thorns, and brambles, and rocks on the road. But God himself clears the way. We will be all right."

"And Joshua? Why was he singled out? Will he be all okay?"

"Well, as to that, he will have to tell you himself."

"Oh." Kirsten shook her head and began to wheel a laughing and smiling Malachi out the door backwards. "We have not spoken in months. Not since I began to see Brandon . . ." She stopped herself and waved her hand in the air. "We just haven't seen each other. He doesn't come to the diner anymore and I haven't been to his forge with Malachi, so . . . I just hope he is all right. I'm grateful for what he did on Friday. Please tell him that the next time you see him."

"Surely you can tell him that yourself," replied Lydia. "It is not hard to find your way to his smithy."

Kirsten was wheeling Malachi out to the road. "No. Those days are over. All my Amish days are over. I told you that last week. Thank him for me. *Danke*."

The evening was beautiful. The light was warm and golden. She spoke with Malachi, messed his hair and teased him, and pointed out a meadowlark on a fence post. In her mind, three faces jostled for her attention: Ty, Brandon, and Joshua. She worked to focus her thoughts on Ty and ignore the other two. Brandon was on the road and she had no idea what she thought about him anymore after he had bailed on the funeral. Joshua was Amish and, thankful as she was for what he and the others had done on Friday at the procession, she was done with the Amish. They did not want to include her in their church, so she did not want to include them in her life, over and above helping to care for Malachi.

Her heart shrank a bit as she thought everything through. Ty was dead and buried. Brandon might not be the kind of man she had convinced herself he was. Joshua and the Amish were no longer part of her future. It looked like a lot of dead ends to her, where months before she had felt she had unlimited options and opportunities. Her mood sank with the sun. There didn't seem to be much to look forward to. She wished she could wheel Malachi along the dirt road into the sunset for a hundred years.

But that Saturday night there was a knock on the door. She expected Brandon, who had not texted or called since he'd left, and she also expected flowers, and a card, and apologies, and if he really felt he needed to make up to her, a big chocolate bar. When she swung the door open, there were no flowers or chocolate bars or cards. There wasn't even a Brandon.

Instead it was a young Amish man, a straw summer hat in his hands, looking perplexed, and troubled, and out of place.

"Joshua." She didn't know what else to say. "Joshua."

He managed a small smile. "So, I was wondering if you would like to go for a buggy ride."

Chapter 8

$\mathcal{F}$ive minutes after saying yes, the buggy rolling along the edge of a roadway as cars and trucks whizzed past, Kirsten wondered what had possessed her to agree to spend the evening with Josh Miller. Neither of them were speaking as the buggy surged ahead – Kirsten felt awkward about the fact that Joshua had been publicly rebuked because of his desire to support her in her grief, and she felt doubly awkward about the matter because she hadn't wanted his support, and triply awkward because she had no desire to like him for doing what he did. She turned away from him to watch children playing soccer in a schoolyard – she supposed she could say she felt even more awkward than all of that because she had the totally irrational idea he knew about the absurd daydreams she had indulged in about him. Their kissing, him falling in love with her – insanely in love – imagining them romancing one another in the highlands of Scotland . . . Without thinking, she growled and spat over the side of the buggy, disgusted with herself. What would he think of her if he had known?

"Are you ill?" asked Joshua, slowing the glossy black mare. "Are you all right?"

She scowled at the ditch that ran alongside the road. "I'm sorry the bishop gave you such a hard time on account of me."

"The bishop?"

"You know what I mean, Joshua. You were at the funeral procession for Ty. And Bishop Yoder called you out on account of that. It meant . . . it meant a lot to me to see you there . . . you and the others . . . but I wish you hadn't gotten into trouble because of it."

"Oh, man is born to trouble as the sparks fly upwards. It is nothing new for me. I have broad shoulders."

"Still."

"I would do it again."

"You would do it again." Kirsten repeated his words and turned back to look at his face. The golden sunset streaked his features. "You mean that? Knowing you could get into even worse trouble?"

He shrugged. "In this world, you will have much trouble."

Despite her desire to give Joshua absolutely no encouragement at all, she could not prevent a small smile from curling up one side of her mouth. "You and your Bible quotes."

"But be of good cheer, Kirsten. I have overcome the world."

"Oh." Now she grinned. "You have? Personally?"

"Well . . . with some help from the Lord."

"Ha." She laughed. "*Some help?*" She pointed to a dirt track just ahead of them. "Can't we take that? Does it go anywhere?"

"To a pond, sure. But it is a rough track."

"*Gut.* Because it's the road to hell that's paved."

He looked at her in astonishment, his mouth open, but nothing coming out.

"So?" She widened her brown eyes at him. "I can make jokes and quote quotes too."

It was definitely a rough track. They bounced, and jerked, and swayed, and once she almost pitched headfirst into the mare. But she had asked Joshua to take it, so she had no intention of wavering in her decision or whining. She commented on the dairy cows that a young girl and boy were bringing in for the night, then on a swarm of fireflies, then on the appearance of the first star in a sky still pale blue.

"Star light, star bright," she began and stopped.

"Don't you know the rest of it?" he asked.

"I've known the rest of it since I was three years old."

"So?"

"So, you're Amish."

"So?"

"So, some of you don't like . . . things that aren't strictly religious."

"Like ice cream, and jelly beans, and pink lemonade?"

Again, she smiled despite herself, but kept her eyes fixed straight ahead. "Exactly."

"First star I've seen tonight," he recited. "I wish I may, I wish I might, have the wish I wish tonight."

It made her laugh again. "Okay, Mister Amish Know Everything. What is your wish?"

"But it's not my wish to make. You saw the star."

"Yes, I saw the star, the first star I saw this evening . . . though now there are nine or ten or twelve. But it was the first star you saw too. So, what is your wish?"

"I have to tell you?"

"*Ja.* That is the game."

"Whose game? Who made up these rules?"

"I did. Malachi Schrock and I did. It's an old Pennsylvania Dutch game that we have modernized."

"Ah, but we Amish don't like modern."

Kirsten arched an eyebrow. "And that's why you have rubber tires on your buggy wheels?"

"Ha." He was grinning. "Okay, I will play your modern version of an old Pennsylvania Dutch game."

"Good. And your wish is?"

"Are you looking for a particular answer?"

Kirsten maintained innocence, while inwardly kicking herself for having started what they both knew was a playful flirt. "Any answer at all will be fine. So long as I get one."

Joshua began to whistle. "Well, well, well. So, let me see . . ."

She listened to his low, musical whistling for over a minute before blurting out, "You mean, you don't know?"

"There are many choices a man can make."

"For heaven's sakes, choose one. Seriously."

"If I choose one, I cannot choose another."

"Yes, life is about making choices. Wishing is about making choices too."

"Hmmm."

"Hmmm, yourself. Out with it. You could have shoed a matched pair of Percherons by now."

He glanced at her as the dark began to drape her face and her shoulders. "Did you like that?"

"Like what? Did something just happen?"

"Did you like watching me shoe the Percherons?"

She refused to meet his gaze. "I enjoyed seeing the Percherons, yes. They're very powerful and very beautiful."

"That's not what I asked you."

"And that's not what I asked you. Come on, Josh. You're totally stalling. Star light, star bright. What's your wish? Then we can talk about the Percherons."

"Okay, well, you know, it is not so hard."

"You're acting like it's the hardest thing in the world."

"Friendship." He said it very quietly. Then repeated the word even more softly. "Friendship."

"What?" She'd heard, but wasn't sure she'd heard correctly.

"Friendship. With you. *Ja*. Friendship with you would be very good. Just friendship. I ask for nothing more."

She did not respond for several minutes. The night closed around them like a black fur. "We were friends once."

"Twice."

"Yes, once or twice."

"So, I should like to have the friendship back and maybe keep it for a while. For a good while. If God wills."

Kirsten hesitated. "That isn't such an unreasonable request. You really can be the gentleman. All right. If God wills, then I will. Let's be friends again. And stick to it."

He laughed in the dark. "Amen."

"Amen."

"Are you chilly, Kirsten?"

"Oh, no. The night is as warm as blood. As if God or creation is exhaling. I feel perfectly comfortable. In fact, I feel wonderful."

"I'm glad to hear that. So, then, what is your wish?"

"My wish?"

"Star light, star bright."

She smiled a smile she knew he could not see. "That's my secret."

"Your secret? I must tell all and you must tell nothing?"

"That's how the game is played."

"*Ja*? You're sure?"

"Of course, I'm sure. I modernized it, didn't I?"

"It does not seem to me to be a very fair game."

"Games don't have to be fair to be games."

"No?"

"No." She pointed, but he could not see her point. "Now look at the stars."

It was a clear night, without a moon, so the stars were everywhere and gleaming, Kirsten thought, like thousands upon thousands of silver rings, rings that someone had spent an eternity polishing, rings of the finest and most expensive sterling silver.

"When I consider thy heavens, the work of thy fingers, the moon and the stars, which thou hast ordained, what is man, that thou art mindful of him?" Joshua recited quietly. *"And the son of man, that thou visiteth him? For thou hast made him a little lower than the angels, and hast crowned him with glory and honor."*

"O Lord our Lord, how excellent is thy name in all the earth," Kirsten whispered in response.

Joshua stopped the buggy and sat back, staring at a sky strewn with sparkling points of light. "So, this is something, really something. I have not seen a night like this for months. Not since Christmas."

"There is so much light you can hardly see the darkness between the stars."

"Ja. See how white the Milky Way is."

"You could almost drink it."

Joshua laughed at that. "Sure. It would be a good drink too."

Kirsten did not want to say the next words that came out of her mouth, but the urge was irresistible. "This is a special night. A very special night."

"A good night for reviving old friendships."

She smiled and she knew he could see her smile in the brightness of the starlight. "Yes, it's a very good night for that."

"You know . . ."

But Joshua did not get an opportunity to finish his sentence. In an instant, cascades of purple, and green, and crimson light fell down through the sky, obscuring the stars with an overwhelming brilliance. For a few moments, the night was a waterfall of color that flashed and pulsated as if it were alive. Then the colors changed to white, and silver, and began to loop in and out of each other, to swirl in circles, to roll up and over fresh curtains of light that dropped from the heavens. Kirsten would look back and call it the night she kept saying or doing things she didn't want to say or do and now came another of them – impulsively, caught up in the beauty of the display spread before them, she reached over and seized Joshua's hand.

"Oh, Josh," she said, hardly raising her voice. "What is this? I have never seen the Northern Lights."

He squeezed her hand. "Once before, when I was about nine, I remember them. They were white that time, all white, and they moved around like whirling ropes in the sky. It was November because we were burning leaves and roasting potatoes underneath them. But colors like this? Like a rainbow in the night? I can't believe it."

"The heavens declare the glory of God and the firmament showeth his handiwork," Kirsten said, eyes fixed on the waves and undulations of brightness. *"Day unto day uttereth speech, and night unto night showeth knowledge. There is no speech nor language where their voice is not heard."*

"Their line is gone out through all the earth, and their words to the end of the world," Joshua continued. *"The law of the Lord is perfect, converting the soul. The testimony of the Lord is sure, making wise the simple."*

Kirsten did not remove her hand from Joshua's. *"The statutes of the Lord are right, rejoicing the heart. The commandment of the Lord is pure, enlightening the eyes."*

Joshua nodded. *"The fear of the Lord is clean, enduring forever. The judgments of the Lord are true and righteous altogether."*

"More to be desired are they then gold, yea, than much fine gold."

"Sweeter also than honey and the honeycomb."

Kirsten continued. *"Moreover, by them is thy servant warned and in keeping of them there is great reward."*

Joshua was silent a few moments, watching the lights turn golden, and flash from one end of the sky and back again, like children playing, or like rainbow trout darting up and down a bright and translucent stream. Then he murmured, *"Let the words of my mouth, and the meditations of my heart, be acceptable in thy sight, oh Lord, my strength and my redeemer."*

All this made Kirsten happier than she had felt in weeks, and happier in a different way than the happiness she had felt with Brandon or even Ty, years ago before he had been deployed. Obviously, the carpet of stars had added to her feeling of joy, and now the *aurora borealis* had taken her over the edge. But the warm strength of Joshua's hand – there was no point in denying it – added as much or more to the astonishing buggy ride as the heavenly light show did, and his calm, sturdy voice reciting the Scriptures with her made her feel a peace, and a sense of being safe and secure, that had eluded her for years since Ty's departure. She was in no hurry to go home, in no hurry to stop looking at the ribbons of light rippling across the night, and in no hurry to take her hand back. She would just have to risk him getting the wrong idea.

And what would the wrong idea be? That she liked him? That she trusted him? That she felt amazing sitting there beside him under the dancing sky? That they were friends again? All of it was true, so let him think what he liked. Kirsten was in no hurry to change anything about her evening buggy ride with Joshua Miller.

Finally, the Northern Lights faded and the stars returned, spilling like the purest well water in a silver torrent through the blackness. Gently,

Kirsten withdrew her hand, but made a point of smiling kindly at Joshua as she did so. He apologized for the lateness of the hour – it was past midnight – and she told him she didn't care. *If only every night in my life were like this, Josh,* she said, but not to him. *If only this night repeated itself over and over again through all eternity.*

Joshua's buggy had lamps encased in glass on either side of the front seats, candles, that he lit before they started back. There were two more at the back of the buggy, larger and brighter, as well as an orange triangle that would reflect headlights, so that they would be safer in traffic. But he decided to take back roads as much as possible, and they were only on the paved roadway for five or six minutes, during which time only two cars passed them, and passed them slowly. Neither of them spoke as they drove back from the dirt track where they had watched the *aurora borealis,* but for Kirsten it was not an uncomfortable silence. She almost reached for his hand again, but this time resisted. They had had enough intimacy for one evening. She did not want things to move too quickly, if in fact they had moved anywhere at all. But there was no denying it had been one of the most beautiful nights of her life.

He parked at her door. "*Guten Nacht,* Kirsten. I hope it was a wonderful evening for you in the company of Gretchen the mare and myself, the Amish farrier."

"Well, Josh, it was kind of an unforgettable night, wouldn't you agree?"

He nodded. "Such nights come along once in a lifetime. Who knows when we will see Northern Lights like that again? Perhaps never. So, we must hold on to the experience."

"Hold onto the memory. Yes."

He came around and helped her down from the buggy. She waited for him to do that rather than climbing down on her own. Their hands touched briefly. She smiled up at him in her bling blue jeans, and gray hoodie, and tan cowboy boots.

"Maybe you'll start coming by the diner again?" she asked.

He smiled. "Maybe."

"I mean, you still drink coffee, right?"

"I am a blacksmith as well as a farrier. So, it is required."

"And eggs? And bacon? Flapjacks? You used to."

"I still do when I am hungry."

"So, come hungry."

"I promise."

"Cook has made a new breakfast special that he calls Zook Meets Yoder. You have to try it. There's blood sausage and potato pancakes along with everything else an Amish man could want. But you'd have to be starving before you ordered it."

He grinned and shrugged. "I can come starving. That's easy. I am at the smithy at five and if I come to the diner at eight I will be ready to eat a horse."

"A Percheron?"

"Maybe a Percheron. So, then I will be more than ready to ask the waitress for a Yoder and Zook."

"Be sure that you do. And be sure it's the right waitress."

"There will be no mistake there."

"Good."

In her room, she brushed out her hair and looked at the stars through the window. She went over the night again and again, every single word, every little gesture. What had the night meant to him? Was he thinking about it right now or was he fast asleep? She knew what the night meant to her. It was more than unforgettable. It was an omen.

She was not the sort of person who looked for omens in everything unusual that occurred nor did she expect them. But Northern Lights while they sat in a buggy together for the first time in months? She shook her head as she used her brush, one hundred times to each side. No, it had not been a coincidence. They were meant to be together and they were meant to see the lights together. So . . . what did it mean?

Friendship. All right, yes, friendship, a friendship renewed. More than friendship? Oh, who could say? She was confused about men and relationships. Ty was in her head, and Brandon – he could be so sweet – and now Joshua was back, jostling for a place in her daydreams and her night time thoughts.

Would he show up at the diner in the morning? That would tell her something. What would she feel if he did? What would she feel if he didn't? Maybe she'd feel relief if he didn't come through the door and order Zook Meets Yoder. Or she might feel devastated after the night under the stars they'd shared together. She might even be angry. She might call him up on the phone and give him a piece of her mind – *How can you not come to the diner after last night? Didn't our time together mean anything to you? I thought you cared about us becoming good friends again?*

But he didn't have a phone.

Kirsten turned out the light and put her pillow over her head.

"I don't want any dreams," she said into her sheets and blankets. "No dreams about anyone. Not Ty, not Brandon, and not Joshua Miller. Tomorrow will be what tomorrow is. I can't make it come any faster by thinking about it, or wondering about it, or even praying about it. It already is what it is. I'll wake up, and go to work, and tomorrow will be what it is."

She slept like a stone. Too much like a stone because she was almost late, and trying to eat toast and jelly with one side of her mouth, while brushing her teeth on the other side. She threw on new jeans that were dark indigo with absolutely no bling, tugged on her cowboy boots, tossed on a white top with three buttons at the throat, and ran out the door. Her shift started at six-thirty and she pulled into the parking lot at Zook's Diner at six twenty-eight. She flew in the back door, and out to the counter, and began taking two truckers' orders right away. One of the other girls called out to her as she raced through the kitchen, "Hey, Sparkles, big night last night or something?"

"Or something," Kirsten called back.

"Did you see those Northern Lights?" one of the truckers asked her when she handed him his plate of ham and eggs. "Weren't they something?"

The door jangled and Joshua walked in an hour early. A huge rush swept through Kirsten and she smiled from ear-to-ear.

"Yeah," she replied. "They were something."

Chapter 9

July
Sunday evening,
Philadelphia, 10:35 PM

𝒯he rest of July, for Kirsten, was a twister.

Brandon surged back into her life, predictably, with cards, flowers, and chocolate bars. There were four or five trips to Philly in his rig. Nice restaurants. Good movies with popcorn and Coke. Sweet walk and talks in the Lancaster parks. Even visits to Ty's grave. Lots of hugs.

But.

Few kisses. Very few kisses. She was confused about kisses. Confused about which ones she had imagined and which ones had been real. Not just with Brandon, but with Josh too. In Josh's case, she knew she had never kissed him on the lips or on the cheek. Ever. In old daydreams from months before, yes, she had imagined all sorts of kisses and other foolishness. But in real life? Nothing. And she was determined, at least for the time being, to keep it that way.

But.

With Brandon?

There had been lots of kisses. Before Ty's body was recovered. Since then, and since the funeral that Brandon had not attended, not so much and not so many. He was hurt, she could see that, and she didn't know what to tell him. So, she fed him clichés. She needed time. She was still getting over Ty's death. Her emotions were in shambles. She wasn't sure what she thought about being with a man who didn't want a family. And all of this was true.

But.

She knew it wasn't the real reason she didn't want to kiss Brandon. And he knew it too. They both knew the real reason. And one evening, sitting in the rig at a truck stop outside Philadelphia, Brandon, against his better judgment, blurted it out.

"It's that Joshua Miller."

"Don't be ridiculous," she snapped back immediately.

"I know you're seeing him."

"I am not *seeing him*, Brandon. He comes to the diner in the mornings for bacon and eggs or a Zook and Yoder. Am I not supposed to be pleasant to him because I'm dating you?"

"Friends tell me you're back at his smithy."

"*Friends*? What *friends* are those? Do you have a little spy network out stalking me?"

"You're there every week."

"Really, Brandon, when did I stop going to his smithy? I've been taking Malachi there for months. There's nothing new about me taking the Schrock boy to watch Mr. Miller hammer at horseshoes or buggy wheels and make the kind of noise the child delights in."

"Is he my competition?"

She rolled her eyes. "Am I part of a contest now? Am I a trophy?"

"I thought we were an item, Kirsten."

She had no wish to be mean to Brandon, but she couldn't bite her tongue. "You mean, like a can of chicken noodle soup at Walmart?"

"I mean, like I thought we meant something to one another."

She softened. "I like you very much, Brandon. You've been very good to me. But . . . I'm just trying to think things through. Ty's death changed everything and I'm just trying to think things through."

"So, we're not a couple?"

She blew out her breath in exasperation. "Don't push me, Brandon. Please. Just give me some space, okay?"

"No problem." He held up his hands. "No hugs, no kisses, no sweet nothings when we say goodnight to one another. Everything is forbidden."

"If I want you to kiss me, believe me, you'll know about it. If I don't want you to kiss me, you'll know that too, and I want you to respect me and respect my boundaries. Can you do that? Can you do that for me?"

"Sure. But can we keep on seeing one another?"

"Of course, we can keep on seeing one another. When did I ever indicate otherwise?"

"First there was a hurricane of kissing and now there's scarcely one a week."

"Brandon. Please. Back off."

"Okay, okay." His hands went up again. "Backing. All kissing is off."

"I never said all kissing was off. I just need some time. If you care about me, Brandon, give me that time."

He scowled out the front window at the headlights zipping past in the dark. "All right. You can have all the time in the world. But I know this is about your dorky Amish blacksmith. I know you go on buggy rides along with everything else you do with him."

Kirsten could feel her face flush and grow warm. "Your spies again? How many do you employ?"

"Do you want to tell me about the buggy rides?"

"Do I have to? Is it a requirement of our relationship?"

"If you still consider us a couple . . . yeah, it is. How would you like it if I started taking Jessica Kitchens out for midnight rides in my rig here?"

Kirsten stiffened in her seat. "Do whatever you like."

"That wouldn't bother you?"

"I told you. You're free to do whatever you like."

"So, we're not a couple?"

"If you're going to keep on having people stalk me, and then resort to interrogating me about how I spend my time, and who I spend it with, and why . . . then, no, we're not a couple."

"Yeah, yeah, I get it. You're going Amish again."

She sighed. "Believe me, I am not going Amish *again*. I don't even wear my hair up or put on a long plain dress when I go to take care of Malachi Schrock anymore. Joining the Amish faith is one of the farthest things from my mind."

"Buggy rides with the Amish blacksmith aren't."

She had never rolled her eyes at Brandon before and now she performed the second roll of the night.

"Keep it up, Brandon," she warned, "and you will get me taking buggy rides every evening and twice on Sundays."

"And enjoying his kisses," Brandon snarled.

She closed her eyes. "We don't kiss. We've never kissed. It's not like that. We really are just friends. Something you obviously can't conceive of. He never speaks ill of you. Why must you speak ill of him?"

"How else do you want me to speak about the enemy?"

"*The enemy*? This is not Iraq or Syria or Afghanistan. He is a friend. Just a friend. No more, no less. But if you keep pushing, I swear you will make him more. You will drive me to him. Now stop. Just stop. And take me home before you say something else you'll regret."

"Just friends, huh? *Just friends*?"

Kirsten looked out her side window at the darkness. Far behind them were the sprawling lights of Philadelphia. "Take me home. If you have any feelings for me or if you respect me at all right now, Brandon Peters, take me home. Or do I have to beg?"

He turned the keys in the ignition and the big diesel engine began to rumble. "No one needs to beg. Not you. Not me. I'm sorry. Let's limit the damage and get back to Lancaster."

She continued to look out the side window. "Thank you."

He reached for her hand.

She did not offer it to him.

"Okay," he said, putting both hands on the wheel. "Okay."

"Yes," she responded, refusing to look at him. "More than okay."

The inevitable cards, and roses, and candy followed a few days later, the apologies, the regrets, and they kissed – yes, kissed – and made up, and buggy rides, and smithies, and Amish farriers were not mentioned again. Nevertheless, Kirsten couldn't deny it was sunshine in her heart when the diner door jangled and Josh Miller walked in at seven or seven-thirty or, now and then, eight. Even when she didn't feel talkative, she surprised herself by having plenty to say to him. Once or twice a week buggy rides became three or four times a week buggy rides, and weekly visits to the smithy with Malachi went from once to twice or more, as did dinners with the Miller family. She begged off rides in

Brandon's rig to take up more offers of rides in Josh's buggy, with Gretchen the glossy black mare pulling them along.

One Friday evening, feeling torn between Brandon and Josh, she said no to both of them, but then, around eight o'clock, raced over to the Millers in her red and black Chevy pickup almost in a panic, hair disheveled, and knocked on the door, asking for Josh, and asking him if she could change her mind and join him on a buggy ride to the pond, and might ten-year-old Rebecca accompany them? So long as they had Rebecca back by ten or ten-thirty, Mr. Miller smiled, *ja*, that would be more than all right. Rebecca chattered all the way to the pond, all the time they parked at the pond, and all the way back from the pond, and this was perfect so far as Kirsten was concerned. She wanted to be with Josh badly, so badly, but she didn't want to speak more than a dozen words to him, and she certainly didn't want to say too much or take their friendship too far, and Rebecca – who she adored with her lively, happy as a robin, young girly-ness – was the perfect buffer. After that, every Friday night was a buggy ride with all three of them, in fact, every buggy ride until August was what Kirsten laughingly referred to as the *Trio*. If Josh ever suspected why Kirsten suddenly wanted Rebecca – or Becca – as a tag along, he never mentioned it when he had the opportunity to do so, and he had that opportunity every weekday morning at Zook's Diner. He merely smiled, made small talk and joked, ordered his breakfast, ate it, left a fat tip, and kept his deeper thoughts concerning himself and Kirsten, whatever those deeper thoughts were, inside behind closed lips.

The threesome buggy rides were what Kirsten thought she wanted. Until she realized, late in July, that they weren't what she wanted at all. What she really wanted was to know what Joshua was thinking about – what he was thinking about her, about her and him, and about her and him and the future – if there was any future. Yet she was afraid to leave Becca at home, in case a crazy Kirsten MacLeod blurted something by the pond she didn't want to blurt, or thought she didn't want to blurt. So, Kirsten stewed in her bed before sleep, and stewed some more after she woke up each morning, and kept on stewing when Joshua came in for breakfast Monday to Friday at the diner. The stewing only stopped when she was on the buggy rides because the rides were so full of Rebecca – and coal black Gretchen, and the bright green summer landscape, and Josh in his white straw hat, and white shirt, and suspenders, and the brown leather reins in his large, brown, leathery hands – that her mind emptied of all her convoluted attempts to analyze her relationship with Josh Miller.

And what July buggy rides they were. One Saturday afternoon, they rolled slowly past bright yellow fields of canola. It took hours because Josh kept Gretchen to a very slow walking pace. Yellow was Rebecca's favorite color and she drank the experience in. So did Kirsten. Hours of vivid yellow filled her eyes, and filled her mind, and filled her heart. It gave her a feeling of joy.

"Yellow is an exuberant color," declared Becca, making Kirsten smile with her use of such a grownup word. "It's the happiest color, don't you think, Miss MacLeod? I used to believe sky blue or grass green were the most cheerful colors God had given us, but then I thought, *Without the sun, or without yellow, where would blue or green be?* So now I'm settled on yellow as the most important color on earth. Even the full moon, when it rises in the east, and is still low on the horizon, it's yellow too, a beautiful, rich, golden yellow."

"It is a lovely color," Kirsten agreed.

Becca suddenly pouted. "But then I wonder, will there be yellow in heaven?"

"Oh, I'm sure there will be. God invented the hue, after all."

"*Ja,* but it's a different world up there. It's eternal. No time. No earth. Everything is going to be so unlike this planet, you know."

"Are you sure?"

"Well, I'm not sure sure. But I wonder: Will there be new colors in heaven? Colors that don't exist here? Colors that only exist in eternity? I think about such things a lot. What do you spend your time thinking about, Miss MacLeod?"

Surprised by the innocent question, Kirsten felt the heat rise to her cheeks, and she quickly averted her gaze so that it was fixed on the long fields of canola. "Oh, I think about . . . about work, I guess. And about keeping my house tidy and clean."

Becca was disappointed. "Is that all?"

"Well, no . . . I think about Malachi Schrock. About horses and deer. Flowers that grow wild in the ditches. I think about the God who created such beauty and diversity. I think about the trout in the brooks. I marvel at the stars every night."

"Do you ever think about becoming Amish anymore?"

Kirsten's cheeks blazed.

"Hush, Becca," said Joshua.

"What?" asked the young girl with a bit of a whine.

"Hush," he admonished her again. "That is something very private, something between a person and God, something to only be shared when God tells that person to share it."

"Does it have to be that secret?"

"*Ja*, it does."

"Okay. I guess."

Becca pouted and was silent for several minutes. Which meant the whole buggy was silent, except for the slow, measured sound of Gretchen's hooves striking the dirt path. Kirsten refused to take her eyes off the golden fields of canola and Joshua kept his eyes straight ahead. In due time, Rebecca saved everyone by beginning to chatter about Grandpa teaching her to fish. "Sometimes we let them go," she announced, "and other times we eat them," and both Joshua and Kirsten laughed, and the day went back to being as bright and cheerful as the huge crops of canola once more.

Another memorable ride included a Sunday afternoon thunderstorm. The week had been so hot and humid that the heavens were bound to burst, but the Trio chose to go out on a ride after church and lunch regardless. Becca was in charge of two large thermoses of cold lemonade and gave out cups of the precious liquid grudgingly – "It has to last us all afternoon. Gretchen has the water from creeks or ponds, but we have only the lemon drink."

Lightning flashed in a dark black west right after she said this, the thunder grumbled after the count of eight, the wind picked up, and Becca crammed the thermoses under her seat – "Now it is not lemonade weather anyways. Are we going to go under a tree, Joshua?"

"When there is an electric storm? You know better than that, Rebecca."

"But Gretchen will get wet."

"She can use a bath." Suddenly, the sky broke open with a flash, and a two-count roar, and rain slashed horizontally into the open buggy, driven by a fierce wind. "And so can we, apparently."

Rebecca howled with laughter as the cloudburst soaked them. "Oh, this is more fun than a shower. But I need soap."

Kirsten laughed. "I don't think I've been caught out in a thunderstorm like this since I was your age, Becca. It's spectacular. Though I must look a fright with my hair plastered all over my head and my clothes dripping wet."

"Oh, no, you don't look like a fright," Becca chirped, bouncing up and down in her seat in excitement. "You look like an adventure."

"Oh, I do, do I?"

Joshua gave Kirsten his broad, slow smile, rain pouring off the brim of his straw hat and into his blue eyes. "My little sister is right. That's what you look like."

"An adventure?"

"Sure. A perfect adventure. Everything about you is exactly as it should be right now. Nothing ought to be altered. The rain and storm have created a work of art."

A surge raced through Kirsten at his compliment. She blinked at him as the rain struck her eyes, looking to see if he was joking or serious. "Really."

He shrugged, still smiling at her, the slashing rain making him blink as well. "*Ja*. Really." Then he added: "It is something one friend can say to another, can't they?"

She smiled back, water streaming over her face, only one eye open. "Yes. It is."

"We will never be dry again," laughed Rebecca. "Never, never, never, never."

"You wait," replied Joshua. "Once the wind and rain have had their way, the sun will have his, and he will have the final word."

"What does that mean?" asked Rebecca.

"You will see. The storm is almost gone."

In five minutes, the dark clouds had hurried east, dragging the rain and lightning and the booming thunder with them. Then it was sunlight that poured on the Trio, hot and thick and fiery, and a breeze came with it, a warm, steady breeze that dried their clothes and hair in an hour – three minutes less than an hour according to Rebecca – so that they felt they had been washed, and rinsed, and cleansed, and toweled dry, and made new again, as if it were Eden, thought Kirsten, and the sixth day, and God had just created woman and man. Even Gretchen was soon dry and gleaming.

"This has been one of the most stupendous afternoons in my life," Rebecca shouted, raising her arms over her head. "I feel like God has given birth to us or something." She turned to look at Kirsten. "Don't you think so, Miss MacLeod?"

"Kirsten."

"What?"

"Please call me Miss Kirsten. And yes, you're right. I feel like something that never existed before has come into the world with that summer storm." She glanced at Joshua and swiftly glanced away when he raised his eyes to hers. "I feel as new and as bright as all these fields of canola."

"Me too." Rebecca grinned. "That's exactly what we are. Long sweet fields of happiness."

In that precise moment, the sun in her eyes now, instead of the rain, making her squint, Kirsten realized the buggy rides of July had molded her heart in a definite way, and had pointed her soul, like an old red barn's old gray weathervane, in a certain direction, and in no other.

Chapter 10

*K*irsten Macleod didn't look as if she'd tossed and turned all night. Her hair was up and perfect, not a strand out of place, her lipstick was just right, and so was her eyeliner, mascara, and eye shadow. Her jeans fit, her boots fit, her top was modest and comfortable, and she did not look at all flustered rushing about and serving her customers during another morning of Pennsylvania heat and humidity. But when Joshua came into the diner and told her she looked great, she responded that she wasn't great, and that she'd been up since midnight staring at the ceiling, staring out the window, and staring at her Bible.

"This is your fault," she said quietly, as she poured him coffee. "Maybe not all. But lots. I've got your order of Zook Meets Yoder – a double order. It's in the kitchen. You can grab it on your way out the door."

He stopped lifting his coffee cup to his lips. "I just came in the door."

"Good, and so now you can show me how you go out the door. The back door. I'm talking my break early. We have fifteen minutes to solve everything."

"*Vas?*"

She was halfway across the kitchen. "There's your plate."

It was mounded high with fried blood sausage, potato pancakes, Canadian bacon and a lot more. "It would take ten men to eat this," he complained, holding the heavy plate with both hands.

"Or one Amish farrier."

He stopped as he came through the back door. "So, it's raining."

"So, you're Amish. So, what?" Kirsten's hands were on her hips and she didn't appear to care if her hair got wet. "We've been through this before, right? And the thunderstorm was a lot worse."

"As you wish." He sat on the door stoop, blessed his food, and began to eat while a light rain dripped off his hands, and arms, and hat brim. "So?"

"So . . . we've had a lot of buggy rides lately."

"You're not happy with the buggy rides?"

"I'm very happy with the buggy rides. I'm delirious about the buggy rides. That's the problem."

"You want terrible buggy rides?"

Kirsten rolled her eyes. "I've been avoiding Brandon. It's no big deal to get into his rig and go to Philly anymore. It's no big deal to go anywhere in his rig . . . or with him. Anymore." Her perfect hair had perfectly molded itself to the shape of her head as the rain fell heavier. "I just . . . I just want to be in a buggy. With you."

Joshua stopped chewing and swallowed before he spoke. "And Becca."

"No."

"No?"

"No. Just you.

The rain had ruined her eyeliner, eyeshadow, and mascara. It was all running down her face, she knew it, and swiped at it with her fingers, also knowing that would make it streak more.

"So, you see," she went on, blinking against the raindrops and makeup, "a lot of this is your fault. Me, standing in the rain like an idiot, so no one can hear what I'm talking to you about. You, sitting there and stuffing your face with a twenty-dollar plate of Zook and Yoder, that's on the house because cook knows I'm going crazy. Me, up all night trying to figure out who matters more to me, you or Brandon. You, sleeping like an Amish log all night, and dreaming of horseshoes, and Percherons, and not me."

"Kirsten . . ."

She pointed a rain-drenched finger at him. "So, now out with it. Whether I'm Amish or not. Whether I'm *Englisch* or not. Whether my father, and brother, and fiancé were in the military or not. How much do I matter to you?"

"*Vas?*"

"Is that all the German you know today?"

"Kirsten . . ."

"And is my name all the English you know today? I asked a straightforward question and I want a straightforward answer."

There was a peal of thunder.

Despite the intensity of the moment, she smiled. "And that big roar is your answer, *Herr Miller*?"

But Joshua was not smiling. Or eating.

He put his plate down on the gravel and let the rain pour on it.

Then he got to his feet.

"So, you want to know what I think about you, Kirsten Brittany MacLeod?"

She didn't respond, just stood looking at him while the thunder boomed again, and the wet wind lashed at them. It began to feel like the Sunday thunderstorm in the buggy to her. Except she was not laughing, and that storm, and that day, had not been as important to her as this storm, and this day. She found his serious, unsmiling face, and his height, and his dark rain-struck features a bit ominous and intimidating, but she was determined to hold her ground with him and did not move. Her hands went back on her hips, something she knew she had picked up from her mother and, most likely, the Scottish.

He came towards her.

And cupped her small face in his large forge-darkened hands.

"You mean more to me than anyone," he said, so softly she could barely him above the crash of the rain on metal roofs, and brick buildings, and stones. "You mean more to me than anything."

Tears erupted in her eyes. She could feel them. She doubted he could see them with all the rain sweeping over her face. She gripped one of his hands with hers.

"Oh, yeah?" she asked.

He nodded. "For sure."

"So . . . so . . ."

She couldn't stop crying.

He didn't try to stop her. Just kept her face cupped in his hands while she tugged on his thumb and fingers.

"We could . . . we should . . . do more buggy rides . . . go out by the pond . . ." she managed to say.

"Pack a lunch," he replied.

"Look for a covered bridge."

"Especially if it rains."

She laughed. "I don't know, good things are happening to me during rainstorms this summer."

Finally, he smiled. "We could look for the Milky Way."

"Or find another *aurora borealis*."

"Yes, that would be something, *ja*? Another *aurora borealis*."

"Though, in a way, one was enough. Especially that one. Having only one in a lifetime like that . . . makes it special . . . unique . . . one in a million. You know?"

He kissed her on the forehead. "I do know."

"So . . . we could make plans . . . for Friday nights . . . for weekends . . . for Sunday afternoons . . ."

"Lots of plans."

"And go all kinds of places. And do all kinds of things."

"And sometimes." He grinned. "Sometimes we leave Rebecca at home."

"Oh, yes." Kirsten laughed and threw her arms around him. "Sometimes we leave Rebecca at home."

Saturday evening, Zook's Diner, 8:45 PM

"You'd think you'd get enough of this place." Brandon toyed with the steak on his plate. "We could've gone into Philly."

"I didn't want a long drive," Kirsten responded. "I just wanted to talk."

"We couldn't talk in the rig? Out under the stars? Like we always do?" He cut into his steak with his fork and knife. "Or like we used to do."

"Well, that's what I wanted to talk about."

"What? Parking out under the stars?"

"Why we haven't been doing so much of that lately."

"Lately? It's been more than three weeks."

"Okay. I know. I've been busy."

"Busy?" Brandon spoke while he chewed. "Busy with what? Busy with the Amish?"

"Sometimes. Sometimes with the Amish."

Brandon put his head down and cut some more. With a kind of anger. "So, what's up, sugar pops? What did you want to tell me that you had to tell me in the place where you work all day?"

"I . . . I've enjoyed all our time together, Brandon."

He did not reply. Just kept sawing at his steak, popping pieces in his mouth, chewing, and looking over her shoulder or at other people in the diner. It was crowded.

She went on. "You've been very kind. The cards, the flowers, the chocolate . . . you've been amazing."

"But."

She went silent.

He stared at her. "But."

"Brandon, I'm –"

"Going Amish," he interrupted.

"No, no, not exactly. Maybe I'm thinking about that again, I don't know, but that's not it."

"So . . . you're going out with Amish."

"Yes. Yes, I am."

"The big lunky blacksmith guy."

"He's . . . he's not lunky."

"I'm getting dumped and he's moving in. Am I right?"

"I'm not dumping you."

"Feels like dumping," he growled. "I drive trucks, and I know dumping, and it feels like dumping."

"I'm trying to explain. That's why we're here."

He barked out a laugh. "We're here because it's crowded. We're here because you thought I wouldn't make a scene if you brought me to a place full of people. We're here because the staff know you and have your back in case I lose it."

"I'm not afraid of you losing it, Brandon. You've always been an officer and a gentleman."

"I'm just a lance corporal. No brass on my shoulders."

She sighed. "Look, this isn't easy for me either. You think I don't have some feelings for you? We've been together for months."

"But. It's time to move on. Greener pastures."

"No. It's not like that. I need some space, I need some different space. Maybe I will go Amish again, I don't know, but I do know I'm heading in a different direction than you are."

"A Josh Miller direction."

"It's not just about Josh. It's you and me too. We're not . . . we're not clicking."

"Oh. Clicking. That's what it is. We're not clicking. I was wondering what was missing."

"If you're honest with yourself . . . you know we haven't been hitting it off for a long time."

"Whose fault is that?"

She closed her eyes. "Really, Brandon, I'm not trying to find fault."

"Oh, I know that. I know. You're trying to find the thing that makes the clicking sound."

"I just want to be friends."

"Hey. There's an original line. No guy that's been dumped has ever heard that line before."

"I told you. I'm not dumping you. I'm trying to explain. I'm trying to go easy on both of us. I'm trying to say I still like you, and respect you, and that I care about –"

"Okay, listen. I don't need your like. I don't need your respect. I don't need your friendship."

He leaned forward and hissed in her face: "And I sure don't need your pity."

"I don't pity you, Brandon. Please try and hear me out."

"Why? What else do you have to say?"

"I –"

"That you want us to get together for coffee on the second Tuesday of every month? That you want me to meet Josh Miller because you're sure we'll get along? That you hope I'll still visit Ty's grave with you and honor his memory? Be a friend of the family? The new and fabulous Miller and MacLeod family of Lancaster County, Pennsylvania? The family with forty-five kids and more on the way next week?" He straightened in his chair, glowering at her, his face a crisscross of lines, and wrinkles, and rage. "That's what killed us in the end, isn't it? The Amish love big families with piles of kids, and Brandon Peters doesn't want any kids at all. So, give the boot to the Marine, and open the door wide for the lunky Amish blacksmith. And why? Because he's smarter, or better looking, or more fun to be with, or he has acres of money? Nah. Because he'll turn you into a baby factory. That makes him a man."

"Brandon!" Her face immediately flushed with blood and heat. "Don't talk that way to me. Don't you ever talk that way to me."

"What does it matter what I talk like or don't talk like to you? We're over, and I'm yesterday's Facebook post. Kirsten and Brandon are a memory. It doesn't matter what I say. I don't really exist. Hey, maybe I never really did when it came to you."

"How can you say that after all the time we've spent together?"

He got up. "I can say it because all of a sudden, I'm not here at Zook's with you. All of a sudden, I'm not in your life. All of a sudden, I'm a ghost. And a ghost is invisible."

Brandon stalked out of the diner. A number of people turned their heads, and watched him go, and then looked back at Kirsten. Waitresses glanced over at her, and caught her eye, and she shook her head, and half-smiled that it was okay. But it wasn't okay. She'd rehearsed what she'd wanted to say to Brandon all Friday and, in the end, nothing had worked out as she'd planned. Half of what she'd wanted to tell him hadn't come out, and his reaction to what had spoiled even the few thoughts she'd managed to express. She sank her head on one hand and let the tears come.

"I'm sorry, God," she whispered, her lips trembling, "this isn't the ending I wanted, and it isn't the new beginning I wanted either."

Kirsten's home, 1:12 AM

Kirsten stared at a very haggard face in the mirror.

Sleep wouldn't come. She kept replaying the disaster of an evening with Brandon and wondering what she could have said or done differently. Maybe they should have gone to Philly and talked in his rig. Maybe they should have parked under the stars. Maybe breaking up with a man she'd once adored, at a place where she waited on tables, wasn't the brightest idea she'd ever come up with.

Or maybe she shouldn't have talked to him at all. Maybe she should have slept on it. Maybe she should have slept on the whole buggy rides with Josh thing. Maybe there shouldn't be a Josh Thing at all. Maybe there should just be a Brandon Thing. Maybe breaking up with Brandon was a huge mistake, the hugest mistake of her life, and maybe it wasn't God's plan, or his plan for the unfolding of the Universe, for her to be with Josh or the Yoder Amish.

You can always change your mind.

I know.

I mean, that's kind of a birthright thing.

I don't want to change my mind, and then a week later regret I changed it, and try to change it back again.

So, sleep on it.

I can't sleep.

Walk on it.

I don't feel safe walking this late. Or this early. Whichever it is.

Drive on it.

I don't feel like getting behind the wheel either. I'm exhausted.

Okay then. How about a midnight buggy ride?

What? Are you insane?

Well, I'm connected to you, so, yeah, maybe.

I'm not going to go over to Josh's house at this hour and ask him to take me on a buggy ride. What will his parents think? What will Rebecca think? What will Josh think?

Who cares? If you need to do it, just do it.

Part of me is saying that maybe I should be getting away from Josh and getting back with Brandon.

One sure way to find out, girl.

I'm not going to do it.

Fine. Sit here and look at your face in the mirror then. Whoop-de-doo.

What do you want from me? To knock on his door at one o'clock in the morning? Throw pebbles at his window like some sixteen-year-old with a crazy kind of crush?

Aren't you crazy crushing on him?

It's ridiculous. The whole thing is ridiculous. This whole night has been ridiculous. My whole life has turned ridiculous.

The first pebble did not wake him up. She wasn't even sure it hit the window pane. The next six or seven had no effect either.

"In the movies it happens right away," she grumbled.

She put her hands on her hips and glanced around her, looking for inspiration. Or a bigger pebble.

And saw the ladder.

"No," she said out loud. "Insane."

It was tall enough to reach the roof, so getting to Josh's bedroom window was not a problem.

Since she had already gone this far, rapping on his window with her knuckles was not a problem either. A tired face with messy black hair suddenly stared out at her. He lifted the window up.

"Kirsten," he said.

She shrugged. "Yeah, Kirsten. Crazy Kirsten."

"*Vas*?"

"There you go with your limited German vocabulary again. You really need to do something about that. *Bitte*, is a good word for instance. So is *ich*. So is *dich*. So is *liebe*, for that matter. If we ever get that far."

"What are you doing propping a ladder against my window at . . . at . . ."

She helped him out. "Two in the morning."

"What can be so important? What is wrong? Are you in some sort of trouble? What do you need?"

"I am in trouble. I'm in a lot of trouble. My head is spinning. And so is my heart."

Seeing him, her universe seemed to correct itself, and she knew exactly what she felt, and exactly what she needed to do. She reached through the window with her hand and ran a finger down the side of his bewildered face. And smiled.

"Now is the right time for a buggy ride. It's not just my idea of a right time. It's God's idea too."

Chapter 11

August
Monday morning,
Zook's Diner, 8:00 AM

*J*osh was late for his breakfast Monday morning.

But Brandon was early.

He had been sitting, and drinking coffee, and brooding in a booth far away in a back corner serviced by Lily, an older waitress, before Kirsten arrived at work at six-thirty.

Seeing him, her stomach began to cramp.

She knew Pennsylvania thunderstorms, and a big one was brewing in that booth, spoiling to cut loose, and hurl lightning bolts, and it just needed one final ingredient to trigger the blast.

Which was provided at eight minutes after eight when Josh Miller entered the diner.

Brandon's face became even more of a thunderhead.

Josh looked at Kirsten, smiling, a smile that faded when he saw the anxiety cutting into her face. And when she glanced at Brandon in his booth, and he followed her glance, and saw what she saw, he hesitated. Stopped walking towards her. Thought a moment.

And then, in an instant, she saw his mind was made up.

He marched directly to Brandon's corner booth.

"Brandon Peters," he said.

Brandon looked up from his coffee and glared at him. "Go away."

"Lance Corporal Brandon Peters."

Kirsten watched Brandon narrow his eyes. "What do you want?"

"A number of us have wished to go to Ty Samson's gravesite."

"A number of us? A number of who?"

"Yoder Amish. We attended the funeral procession. We watched them bury the casket. But we have never approached his grave."

"So, what's stopping you?"

Josh removed his broad-brimmed straw hat. "We want to honor him. We want to do it properly."

"You don't need me for that."

"We do. You are a soldier. A Marine. Like Sergeant Samson. We know nothing about soldiering."

"That's for sure," Brandon sneered. "You don't even know how to fight for your own freedom."

"*Ja*, we do. It's just we do not use guns or bombs. We use prayer. The Bible. Sermons. Hymns. And some of us, a few, have learned to honor those who fight for freedom in a different way than we do. No, we do not honor the killing or the weapons or the brutality of the warfare. But we honor the sacrifice. We have learned to honor that very much."

Brandon did not respond.

"Help us." Josh's voice became a kind of plea. "Help us honor your friend. Help us honor all those who have sacrificed. Help us to do it as it should be done." He paused. "Help us to honor you."

Brandon's eyes locked on Josh's.

Kirsten heard everything, despite the growing noise of the breakfast crowd. She watched Brandon's face work – muscles tightening, and relaxing, and tightening again. Watched Josh remain at Brandon's booth, perfectly straight, perfectly still, arms at his side, as if, she thought, he was himself a Marine on guard at the Tomb of the Unknown Soldier. She wondered if Brandon might not pick up on this. She was sure he would. She still knew the kind of man he was.

And Brandon suddenly nodded. "I know you are not comfortable with flags or guns. But you are all right with flowers and wreaths and prayers."

"Yes," Josh responded.

"These people of yours. These Yoder Amish. Bring your flowers. Bring your Bibles. Bring your prayers. Meet me at the entrance to the cemetery at ten. Is that too soon?"

Josh smiled. "No. No, it is not too soon. We shall be there. *Danke*, Lance Corporal."

"*Bitte* . . . Amish farrier."

A ghost of a smile passed over Brandon's face and was gone.

Kirsten begged off work till noon, explaining what was unfolding to the cook, and raced home to change. Josh had not stayed behind to chat or eat breakfast, but had left the diner without a word to her. She knew he had gone to gather the families who wished to be part of a prayerful graveside ceremony. She slipped on her plainest ankle-length dress, put her long brown hair up into a bun, tugged on a pair of black shoes that could have been stitched together in the 1880s, fished out a black bonnet she only used for Amish funerals, and was at the cemetery by ten to ten.

Three or four buggies were already parked there and Amish in funeral black, including the men with their black felt hats and the women in large black bonnets, stood quietly by the front gate. She saw the Schrocks and the Millers – Rebecca risked a quiet smile – and another family she knew were the Reimers, who had come over to the Yoder Amish from the Old Order Mennonite community. Without greeting anyone – though she did muss Malachi's hair playfully – keeping her eyes down, Kirsten joined them. She did not see Josh anywhere. Or Brandon.

Both of them arrived five minutes later in a Hummer painted dark green. Brandon was in uniform, Josh in sold Amish black – even his hair looked darker than usual. They emerged with a chaplain in tow, actually two – one Kirsten recognized as a local Catholic priest, the other was in a Marine uniform and had a distinctly Protestant air about him. Josh was carrying a simple wreath of white roses. As the group of them began to walk in procession into the cemetery, Josh and Brandon and the two ministers at the front, Kirsten noticed that others were carrying flowers as well. Lydia Schrock had a red rose. Adam Schrock a pinkish one. Malachi had both colors in his lap as they wheeled him forward. Others held roses from their gardens, or peonies, or even snapdragons and pansies. Rebecca held three bright daisies. Kirsten lagged behind and picked a half-dozen wild daisies that were growing beside a hedge.

They formed a circle around Ty's grave. Both ministers spoke and read from their Bibles. Both prayed. Brandon had placed a wreath on a stand nearby, apparently well before his arrival with Josh and the pastors, and now he brought it forward and placed it by the gravestone. Then Adam Schrock, head bared, prayed out loud. So did Josh's father. So did Helmut Reimer, the patriarch of the Reimer family. Once those prayers were done, Josh placed his white wreath next to Brandon's, and everyone stepped forward, and placed their flowers by the stone carved with Ty's name, and rank, and date of birth, and date of death.

After that, Adam Schrock led out in two old Amish hymns, both in German, slow, and ponderous, and – Kirsten thought – magnificent. She picked up that the hymns spoke of suffering, and death, and faith, and persecution, and the glories of the life to come. Then the women, and the men, and the children clasped the hands of the two ministers, but they especially clasped hands with Lance Corporal Brandon Peters, and lingered with him, and spoke quietly to him, and blessed him. Once that was done, Kirsten watched Brandon and Josh shake each other's hands. As people began to leave the cemetery, and horses whinnied and snorted, and harness jangled, Brandon took Kirsten's hand and led her aside under some elm trees.

"Your cheeks are wet," he said. And smiled. "Our Kirsten's been crying again."

Kirsten half-laughed. "She has, hasn't she? You'd think she'd have run out of tears by now, between one thing and the other."

"Well, I wanted to tell you I'm not going to be the one to cause you anymore tears or heartbreak. If the Amish turn out to be the sort of people you really do want to spend the rest of your life with, God bless you. If Josh turns out to be the sort of man you want to spend the rest of your life with, God bless him. I won't interfere. I won't come to Zook's Diner and sit growling in a corner like a bad-tempered lion. I won't come your door at midnight and demand to see you. I go in peace. I give you over to God and the Amish and I hope they'll know what to do with you."

"Oh, Brandon –"

"Hey. What's this? I said I wasn't going to cause you anymore tears."

"You're being so kind, and sweet, and . . . and noble."

"Noble? Me?"

"Yes. Noble, you. You really are an officer and a gentleman. I ought to salute you."

146

"You can't. You're out of uniform."

"I'm wearing my own uniform." She kissed him on the cheek. "That's how I salute."

"It's a pleasant salute." He gave her a quick hug. "I'm taking off. I'm on the road tonight and taking a load into Mexico."

"Oh. Be safe."

"I will."

"And . . . Brandon . . . we'll see you around?"

He grinned. "I'll always be around. Take care, Smiles."

"You too. Please."

He was gone.

Halfway between Ty's grave and the gate, Josh stood waiting. As slim, and dark, and steady as an iron sculpture.

She came towards him and grasped his hand.

They began to walk.

Not through the gate, but all around the graveyard.

"What will the bishop say?" she asked.

"Oh, we will be rebuked. Most certainly we will be rebuked. But there were no flags, or guns firing, or marching bands, or patriotic speeches, just prayers, and hymns, and Bible verses – perhaps he will relent. So, but this will be the second warning. I know if he says he must administer a third warning then shunning will follow. It doesn't matter. This was the right thing to do. For your fiancé. For Brandon. Yes, for you and I. But also for the Amish. Before God, it was the *most right* thing we could do. Just as attending the funeral procession was. I cannot go back on either of those things. I cannot sincerely repent. So, if God leads me to other places and other faith groups, well . . ."

"I don't want you to go to other places or other faith groups. I want you here."

"Good."

"Because now we're an item, you know. Now we're this kind of package thing."

"*Ah, ja.* The Package Thing."

"I will want more time with you, not less, from this exact moment on. More breakfasts at Zook's. More visits to your smithy. More Percherons. More buggy rides at all times of the day. More ponds, more covered bridges – if we can find them – more night skies that are full of summer stars, more picnics, more prayers, more of everything."

"I think we can handle that."

She went on. "Perhaps . . . I don't know when . . . I will feel strong enough to approach the bishop again and ask to join the Amish faith. Perhaps he will have softened in his disposition towards me. Perhaps God will have opened Pastor Gore's heart big and wide. I honestly don't know what will happen. But I think I shall try again. When I think the time is right."

"I'm glad to hear that, of course. But no, do not rush things. Give the bishop time to get over what we have done to honor Ty Samson. He will connect all that with you and, I suppose, in a way, he will never forget the connection. But let us have some time so that everything can cool down. That would be best."

"I don't want everything to cool down."

"No?"

"No." She leaned her head on his shoulder. "I don't want us to cool down."

"Oh. I wasn't thinking about us. I was thinking about Pastor Gore and Bishop Yoder and . . ."

"I know what you were thinking about, you lunky Amish farrier. But right now, all I'm thinking about is us. I've had to think about so many things this summer and now all I want to think about is us. That's all I ask for from God now. Us."

Chapter 12

*N*ow Kirsten's life became everything she had prayed it could be.

Josh was at the diner every morning, Monday to Friday. She was at his smithy with Malachi on Monday and Wednesday afternoons. She ate with his family on Wednesday evenings. Her and Josh took walks together, or buggy rides, three to four times a week. If they were both free, Saturday afternoons were set aside for picnics or much longer rides out into the countryside. The same was true for Sunday afternoons, except those always wound up at a hymn sing at one of the larger Amish homes. People were warm and friendly to her at the hymn sings, even Bishop Zook and Pastor Gore, even with a fresh rebuke from the bishop hanging over Josh's head because of the memorial at Ty's graveside, a memorial the bishop knew she had attended with Josh, and where he also knew she had dressed exactly like one of the Yoder Amish.

"The rebuke does not have much teeth," Josh explained to her. "There was nothing patriotic

151

about the memorial, after all. It was, for the most part, a very Amish way of saying goodbye – Amish prayers, Amish hymns, Amish blessings, *ja*, Amish flowers from Amish gardens too. No, the bishop is not that aggravated. He simply felt he needed to say something, but most of our people are glad we blessed a young man who died too soon, regardless of the circumstances in which he died. Bishop Yoder understands we did not honor war at his graveside. That it was imply about honoring him, a person God created and sent his Son into the world to love and redeem."

"So . . . may I attend worship services without feeling censured?" she asked him.

"Yes, of course, if that is what you wish. You can sit with the Schrocks, if you like, or with my mother and the girls. You know the men and women must sit separately, even the boys and girls."

"Yes, I know."

"You have never attended a worship service, have you?"

"Not really. Only a few funerals. I intended to get more involved after I was permitted to join the Yoder Amish in April. But, well, that did not happen, did it?"

Josh kissed her on the forehead. "Next time."

She smiled. "Yes, next time."

"Other Amish meet in homes for worship and only do it twice a month. For the Yoder Amish, it is not so. We meet every Sunday morning, and have a lunch afterwards, and *ja*, we meet in one of the larger houses, like ours, for instance, or the bishop's, or the new family, the Old Order Mennonites, the Reimers'. For the winter, we choose the homes that have a good fireplace or a larger wood stove, ones that throw off a good deal of heat. So, please, begin attending, it will help the leadership look favorably on you. And I hope you will be blessed as well. Best of all, we can have lunch together."

"And go for buggy rides afterwards."

"*Ja*, buggy rides with Rebecca, and Deborah, and Tabitha in tow. They will be insistent if you begin joining us for Sunday services."

"That's fine with me. So long as we have Saturdays to ourselves."

"So, I will ensure we always have Saturday afternoons to ourselves. I will make a bold stand against the loud cries and demands of my sisters."

"*Gut.*" She grinned. "*Das ist gut.*"

And the Saturday afternoons of August were *gut*. Sunshine, thunderstorms, wind, rain, hail, it did not matter. She was with Josh, she was falling more in love with him every day – though she had never told him as much – and her world was gently turning on its axis, and turning properly, and turning, she believed, with God's blessing. There were just a few things still not quite in alignment with that world which kept it from being perfect – Josh had not said he loved her (just as she had not said she loved him, but that was different), and Josh had never kissed her . . . except on her forehead and cheeks, which did not count.

She had daydreamed about his kisses months before. Her silly schoolgirl daydreams, she called them. And then she had shut those daydreams down. Completely and forever. No more daydreams. Now she wanted the real thing, and she wanted memories of the real thing. That she would be happy daydreaming about. But not about kisses that had never been real and had never happened. No more of those. So, she waited. Any day now, Josh would kiss her properly.

Once Brandon graciously bowed out of the picture, she had expected it to occur at any moment. But the moments went by. And the days. And almost the entire month of August. There had even been a glorious full moon and a night as warm as a sunny afternoon. In fact, the yellow moon, fat and large and low on the horizon, had seemed like the sun to her. She had said as much to Josh. Had remarked on how beautiful, and magical, and romantic – she had even dared to use the word *romantic* – the full moon was to her. He had agreed. And put his arm around her as they sat together in the buggy watching it rise. He had hugged her with that long, strong arm. She had leaned her head against his shoulder, convinced the moment had come when Miller met MacLeod, when Amish met *Englisch,* when schoolgirl fantasies became a young woman's reality.

But no. He had pressed his lips to her hair. Her forehead. When they said goodnight, her cheek. That was all. He seemed incapable of going beyond that, no matter how much time they spent together.

Should she tell him what to do? Tell him what she expected of him? Tell him to treat her like the girlfriend she was, the very special girlfriend who had begun to lunch with him, and his family, and the other Yoder Amish every Sunday at noon? Oh, of course not. What would be the point of that? He would be polite, and do what she asked him to do, and she would receive a very polite Amish kiss on the lips, that meant absolutely nothing, except that he was a gentleman, and a well-mannered Amish boy. No, she wanted a kiss he chose to give her, he wanted to give her, he made up his mind to give her, a kiss that had nothing to do with her, or her wishes, but only his, a kiss that showed he cared deeply for her, and that he wanted to express those feelings by placing his lips on hers, and kissing her, not just as a friend, but as a man who was – she hoped – growing passionately and hopelessly in love with her.

Or maybe he wasn't growing passionately and hopelessly in love with her.

Of course, he is, you goose. Look at how he treats you. Like a princess. Like a queen.

Well, the princess needs a kiss. Princesses are supposed to be kissed by princes.

He hugs you.

Yeah, he hugs me.

Remember the morning behind the diner? In the rain? How he told you that you mattered more than anything or anyone?

I remember.

So?

So, what? Nothing has happened since then.

Nothing has happened? What? A thousand buggy rides. A thousand walks in the woods. Starry nights. Full moons. The smithy, evening meals with his family, breakfast every weekday morning, Sunday lunch . . .

Sure, okay, a thousand of everything. A thousand thousand of everything to do with friendship. But not one declaration of love. Not one kiss on the lips.

You haven't told him you love him either.

A woman shouldn't have to go first in these things. A man should lead the way.

Really. How very 1750s of you.

So, I can be an old-fashioned girl. So, sue me.

Your day will come, Lollipops.

Yeah, right, once I'm old and gray he'll figure it out.

Your lunky Amish farrier.

My lunky Amish blacksmith.

Lunky and hunky.

Something has to happen soon. It has to. I've prayed so hard. I've wished so hard. It absolutely has to.

Eventually, he will get it right. Eventually, he will take the risk.

I used to hold my breath. But then I almost asphyxiated. So, now I don't hold onto anything.

Except a dream. As always.

Yeah. Except a dream. As always.

It was almost too hot. In fact, it *was* too hot. The humidex was through the roof and the slightest exertion caused Kirsten to perspire along her hairline. It didn't help that she had taken to dressing Amish now when she was out with Josh, especially when they were with other Amish families, or she was attending services, or hymn sings. Not the prayer *kapp*, but the long dark dress with long sleeves, the leather shoes, her hair up – she didn't mind having her hair up, but the dress, even though it was made out of a lighter cotton, forced her to hunt out the shade whenever they stopped the buggy to look at the view or climb down for a bite to eat. Josh said it didn't matter to him if she looked Amish, particularly when they were alone, but she insisted. At the back of her mind, she had the idea the way she dressed from now on would help her chances with the bishop the next time she met with him and the pastors. They would see she truly was serious about becoming Amish. Not just when she was with Malachi and the Schrocks – she'd always dressed Amish for them – and not just at services or funerals, but whenever she was spending time with anyone who was connected with the Yoder Amish. At work or at home, or out shopping, she was still Plain Jane Kirsten Macleod in jeans and a T-shirt or hoodie, but the rest of time she was Amish, and even her jeans and tops became more and more modest, and she stopped wearing shorts and cutoffs.

"I think maybe you are overdoing it a little," Josh admonished her. "No one expects you to look as much like our women as you do. After all, you are not Yoder Amish, are you? Not yet. So, people cut you some slack. As if it were *rumspringa* for you. When all the rules are relaxed for those connected to our faith, all those who have not come to the place of being baptized, *ja?* No one holds you to the same standards as a member of the Amish faith because you aren't a member of the Amish faith. You have taken no vows. You have not been baptized. So, relax. You are too hard on yourself."

"I still think it may make a difference when I am interviewed by the bishop and the leadership a second time."

"Maybe. Maybe not."

"It can't hurt, Josh."

"No, it can't hurt."

So, when they stopped at an isolated cluster of trees that a river cut through, far from the highways and farms, Kirsten put up with the heat and humidity that Saturday afternoon in order to look the way she felt she ought to look as someone who was dating or courting an Amish man – could she use the term courting when she had never been kissed and he had never told her he loved her? Whatever they were, they were an item, a package, a couple, and she felt better sweating it out in a dark Amish dress than feeling far cooler in a tank top and shorts. Josh, on the other hand, wore his white straw hat and a white shirt with short sleeves.

"That should be called cheating," she told him, as they settled down in the shade with a picnic basket and two thermoses of cold lemonade.

"What?" He poured her a glass of lemonade which she did not sip, but gulped.

"Short sleeves."

He shrugged. "That's the tradition. You could be in short sleeves yourself right now. I told you. No one expects of you what you expect of yourself."

"I'll put up with it. Is there a facecloth in that basket? Did we bring some water?"

"Yes, to the cloth. No, to the water."

"You mean we didn't bring any water to clean up with? Or cool off with?"

"I guess not."

She shook her head and stood up. "May I have the facecloth, please? I'll dip it in the river."

"Be careful."

"Of what? The cloth or the river? It's running slowly enough."

"It's deep."

"I can swim."

He smiled. "Even in that dress?"

She stuck out her tongue. "Even in that dress."

The water felt cold to her warm skin. The sun, beating down on the river as it wound through farmlands, and hayfields, and stretches of woodland, made it shine like sterling silver. She mopped her face and the back of her neck. She rolled her up her sleeves a moment to wipe down her arms. She even squeezed river water on top of her head so that it ran through her hair, and down her neck, and along her forehead and cheeks. It made her feel good. She laughed.

"I suppose I'm all wet and bedraggled now," she said.

"You are wet all right," Josh responded. "But bedraggled is not the word."

"No?"

"No."

"What is the word then?"

Josh was silent for half a minute, his legs drawn up to his chest, and his elbows resting on his knees. A long blade of timothy was in his mouth. He shrugged with one shoulder. "All right. Why not? The word is beautiful."

Kirsten stopped wiping her face with the wet cloth. "What?"

"Beautiful. All shining and beautiful. You are better than the river, or the green fields, or the sky and the sun. You are more than all of them put together."

"Really." Kirsten was so surprised her cheeks flushed. "Where is this coming from?"

He shrugged. "I've been silent and cautious long enough."

"I see. Well, do you have anything else wonderful to say about me?"

He chewed on the long piece of timothy. "I do. You are perfection."

She repeated his words, a bit stunned. "I am perfection."

"For sure." He spread open his hands. "I am helpless when you are around. Half of the time, I can't even think straight. What can I say, Kirsten? I'm in love with you."

Now she was even more stunned. "In love?"

"In love."

"You are in love with me."

"*Ja*, I am in love with you. You know? *Ich liebe dich*?"

"I know *ich liebe dich*."

"*Gut*. So, then, today it applies to you." He laughed and pulled the timothy grass out of his mouth. "Who am I kidding? Today it applies? When was I not in love with you?"

"Josh."

"It's true. I cannot think of a moment I was not in love with you. It's as if there was no beginning and no end. It was always there. Even before I saw you. So, then when I saw you, I understood what the feeling was."

Kirsten stood perfectly still. "I have no idea what to say."

"Say nothing. One day I hope you can tell me that you love me too. But, until then, let us dispense with words for a while."

"What . . . what is that supposed to mean?"

"I will show you what it is supposed to mean."

Brandon's kiss, coming as it did years after she had embraced her fiancé Ty Samson for the final time, had been a beautiful blue summer sky for her, and had turned her inside out. Now, with

161

the river sliding like molten silver behind her, and Josh's hands cupping her face, and the sun striking her closed eyes with its heat, his lips suddenly on hers was meteors and comets, it was shooting stars, it was the Milky Way as white as a Christmas snowfall . . . and after several minutes of a kiss that showed no signs of stopping, it was the Northern Lights all over again. Only this time they were inside her, in her head, in her heart, in her whole body, and they were all the colors, and all the swirlings, and loopings, and twistings, and swift turnings.

She fought for air, found some, kept going, dropped the wet facecloth and curled her arms around his neck, let him draw her in closer and closer, felt his strength, and his gentleness, and let him take her with his kisses far out beyond the moons of Jupiter, and the rings of Saturn, far out beyond her world, and her universe to another realm, another reality, another heaven she had never experienced before. It was an avalanche of sweetness and wonder. It was a waterfall of excitement and delight. There was no point in bringing it to an end. So, she didn't.

Finally, he was resting his forehead against hers, and his thumb was rhythmically and repeatedly stroking her cheek. "Was that all right? Are you okay?"

She sighed and leaned her head against his chest. "Of course, it was all right. Of course, I'm okay." She laughed. "Or maybe not. I think I landed on Neptune."

"Neptune. Well, Neptune, that is far away."

"On the other hand, I'm still in your arms, so it isn't all that bad."

"No?"

"No."

"So, I am glad you like being there."

"Neptune?" she teased.

"Ha. You know, I don't care where you are. So long as it is where I am. So long as I am holding you. So long as I can smell your hair . . . and . . . and . . . touch my lips against the softness of your skin."

"Well, that is where I want you to be too, so it sounds like a plan."

"*Gut.*" He laughed. "You know, I really have run out of words. Not that I ever have that many to begin with. But I find I don't wish to talk."

"Oh? So, what do you wish?"

"To get back to what we were doing."

"Ah. I see. Well, I'm sure I can accommodate you, my handsome Amish farrier. But, before we get back to all that serious business we were involved in, I have a few words, even if you don't have any more left."

"You have words. And what are they?"

She lifted her head and locked onto his deep blue eyes. "*Ich liebe dich.*" She smiled as he smiled. "*Ich liebe dich,* my beautiful man." She reached up and pressed her lips against his. "Now bring me back from Neptune. *Ja,* go ahead and bring me back. But take your time, my man. Take all the time in the world."

Chapter 13

August
Sunday afternoon,
the riverside, 3:33 PM

On Sunday, at the church lunch, the bishop had added to the dreamland Kirsten had been living in since Saturday afternoon by nodding at her, and smiling, and taking one of her hands in both of his, and saying, "My dear, I think it's time we chatted again. Let us see if we cannot find some common ground together, hm? What do you think of that?"

She couldn't believe it. "Oh. Bishop Yoder. That would be wonderful. That would be incredible."

He nodded and smiled some more. "*Gut. Gut.* Tuesday evening at my home would suit you then? Say around seven? The pastors will join us."

"Yes, yes, of course. I will have to speak to the Schrocks about making other arrangements for Malachi's care."

"Of course." He released her hand after giving it a warm shake. "We will see you on the Tuesday evening. The Lord Jesus Christ be with you."

"And with you, Bishop Yoder."

Kirsten bubbled over once she was alone with Josh that afternoon. They had agreed to return to the spot where they had kissed the day before. She swung in circles in his arms as she laughed and talked.

"Why do you think he decided to give me another chance? Because I attend the services and the hymn sings? Because I'm dressing Amish ninety percent of the time? Because people know you and I are, you know . . ."

He grinned as she swung. "Courting?"

"Well, aren't we?"

"That is how the Yoder Amish would see it, *ja.*"

"And so, the bishop is afraid I'll run off with you? And wants to make sure I turn into a true-blue Amish woman first?"

"He might be thinking that."

"So, I'm ready for him. And for Pastor Gore. More than ready."

"Are you?" responded Josh as she stopped swinging in his arms and twirled off by herself. "What makes you ready?"

"I've been reading Amish history. I have. And learning more German – high German and low German. And I've asked Adam and Lydia Schrock to tell me everything they can think of about the Yoder Amish . . . how they are different from the Old Beachy Amish, for instance, or even the Old Order Mennonite. I was buying blood sausage the other day, and I ran into Mary Reimer, and I asked her what was different about the Yoder

Amish, and what appealed to them so much that they felt led to leave the Old Order."

"Huh. It sounds like you have been everywhere."

"*Ja*, I have been. Books from the library. From Amazon. Articles online."

"Soon you will know more than the bishop and the pastors themselves. Be careful when it comes to that. They will not like it if they think you are proud about all you have learned."

"I will be humble."

"*Gut.*"

"But it's not that I'm proud. I'm excited. Excited about all the things I have been discovering about the Amish faith. Excited that they have asked me to sit down with them again. And I thought it would be necessary for me to approach Bishop Yoder, cap in hand."

"It's all right if they see some enthusiasm. But be sure and show them your enthusiasm for God too, *ja*? For the Lord Jesus Christ, for the Bible. That will impress them the most, in addition to your being agreeable to all the Yoder Amish practices and godly principles. Yes, show them how committed you are to the Lord and to the Amish faith. But also, be self-controlled and temperate. They will like that. And come with your cap in your hand. They treasure humility, especially in a woman."

"I hope they treasure it in a man as well. It seems to me I came to them with my cap in my hand last April. And my heart in my mouth too. It did not do me any good."

"You have no idea what good it did you. They could not get past your family's war record."

Kirsten's excitement faded instantly. "I know. So, how will they get past it this time?"

"Well, there have been changes, haven't there? The one pastor had a heart attack and can no longer serve. And another, Pastor Schwartz, it is too bad, he had the farming accident, may God heal him, but he is no longer in a position to serve either. So, then, there are the two new pastors since July – Troyer and Graber – and who knows what they will think about you, what they will say? The change may be for the good and in your favor. I am aware that Troyer, in particular, is fond of bringing in converts from the outside, especially those with no Amish or Mennonite background. He believes it adds a godly and righteous spice to the mix. That it brings us fresh blood that stimulates the entire Body of Christ that is the Yoder Amish. So, he may stick up for you. In fact, I am sure he will."

"And you? You will stay on your knees all evening for me? Praying?" She tugged on his hands. "*Ja?*"

"All evening? No?" He brought her against his broad chest and hugged her. "All day. Morning, noon, and night. I will do everything on my knees – shoeing, hoof trimming, wheel rims, plowshares – and every time I strike with the hammer, I will strike for you with a new prayer."

Kirsten laughed and quickly kissed him on the lips. "If that is the case, God Almighty will be totally preoccupied with me, and your prayers for me, and I cannot fail."

Monday evening,
Kirsten's bedroom, 9:37 PM

Kirsten was sprawled on her bed in jeans and a T-shirt that said AMISH COUNTRY with a black buggy and horse underneath the letters. She was typing words into the Notes app on her iPhone:

On Tuesday night –
No eyeliner
No mascara
No eyeshadow
Plain nails
NO hairspray
No lipstick or gloss
No makeup of any kind
No perfume
No jewelry (necklace, earrings, rings, bracelets)
No watch
No mobile in my pocket
No purses
Fresh breath (mints?)

Now and then she glanced at a piece of paper propped up on her pillows and filled with her neat cursive:

Yoder Amish are characterized by –

Swiss origins (not Dutch like the Mennonites)

Clasping their hands in a distinctive way during public prayer (one hand over another, but then both hands are inverted or turned upside down together)

Having hymns other Amish groups do not have which emphasize, more than is usually the case, suffering, loneliness, persecution, and the Cross of Christ

Saying amen three times in a row during public worship and prayers – this is to signify the Trinity

The men cannot have beards until marriage and the beards must be kept trimmed until they are grandfathers – then their beards should not be trimmed

All baptisms must be done in running water in a natural setting – brooks, streams, rivers – no indoor baptisms, and none in a tub or tank of any kind, and none in lakes or ponds

Knocking on another Yoder Amish door must be done three times – rap, rap, rap – again, to signify the Trinity

While a young woman is a virgin and unmarried, she wears a white kapp on her hair, which is always done up in a bun – once she is wed, she changes to a black kapp – when she is a grandmother the kapp may remain black or be exchanged for one that is deep purple or burgundy

All buggy wheels must have rubber rims

All footwear must be of leather and handmade with the exception of rubber boots

Women may only trim their hair to get rid of split ends, it cannot be cut or shortened unless there are medical reasons – men, on the other hand, must always wear their hair short and at least three inches above the ears

No photography

No paintings

No secular music

All undergarments, all bedsheets, all pillowcases must be made of cotton – all clothing must be made of cotton or wool or both – jackets or coats made be made of genuine leather or cowhide

I'm missing a few things.

As if they are going to ask you all that.

Who knows?

They didn't last time.

Well, last time there were two other pastors who aren't there anymore. So, do you have a crystal ball that can tell me what the new ones are going to ask? What if Pastor Troyer asks me to show him how I would hold my hands during public prayer? What if Pastor Graber says, Okay, tell me everything you know about Jacob Amman? And the Swiss influences on the Yoder Amish?

Really, they aren't going to go there.

So, where are they going to go?

Wherever they start, whatever they ask you, they will eventually end up at the same place.

You know that. Your father was in the military, your brother was in the military, your fiancé was in the military. It makes no difference how well you answer their other questions. It will all come down to that.

So, let it.

Of course, now you've added some other fun stuff into the mix. You're dating Joshua Miller, the blue-eyed blacksmith . . .

Courting.

And you coaxed Yoder Amish into attending not only Sergeant Ty Samson's funeral procession . . .

I didn't coax anyone.

. . . but also into taking part in a graveside memorial for the sergeant two months after his internment. A patriotic event.

Oh, for pity's sakes. Get a life. It was not a patriotic event. It was a religious event, a spiritual event, it was prayers and hymns and Bible readings. There wasn't one flag and there wasn't one gun.

There were two uniforms.

So, what. That's the clothes they wear during ceremonials. No one even said, God bless America.

Gore will go after you on the funeral and the memorial.

Let him. I'm ready for him. I'm ready for all of them. I'm ready if they ask about baptism, three knocks on the door, Ty being a Marine, rock and roll, and my split ends.

I don't know why you're going through all this just for one lunky farrier, hot or not.

Because it's not just about one lunky, hunky Amish farrier. It really is a spiritual journey for me. Long before he started orbiting my sun, I wanted to be Amish. I love the quiet. The peace. The slow pace, like a horse walking. No rush, nothing is hectic. You pin clothes on the line to dry, and you use wooden clothespins, like my great grandmother did. Hey, I love the old-fashioned morality too. The Ten Commandments. The Bible in German or King James. No swearing. No blasphemy. And what can beat the slow, slow, slow pace of cooking and baking with a woodstove? Or an absence of the gazillion electronic devices that stress everyone to death outside the Amish community? The long, rolling prayers and the long, rolling hymns . . . they calm my spirit. I come more alive among the Amish. I dream God dreams among the Amish. It's like Jesus is in the chair next to me.

Wooden clothespins and apple pies chilling on the windowsill? If that's what it takes for you to find the meaning of the universe . . .

That's what it takes.

Yeah, well, okay, whatever, sister. Good luck to you.

Yes, well, good luck to you too, sister, since you'll be coming with me.

Huh. I've never figured out how to get out of these things or how to get out of you.

Me neither.

Kirsten leaned over and pecked on her iPhone:

NO chewing gum!

And brush your teeth for five minutes before you leave the house for the meeting ☺

Tuesday evening,
Bishop Yoder's home, 7:00 PM

Demure.

That's what she needed to be at all times with the bishop and the pastors.

Be demure, dress demure, live demure.

Humble and demure.

"Good evening, Miss MacLeod," rumbled Bishop Yoder. "Thank you for joining us. Let us begin with holy prayer."

They all stood.

Kirsten was sure to fold one hand over the other and then invert them.

And, after the prayer, once they were sitting down again, it was the first thing Pastor Troyer mentioned, a broad smile on his face: "I was happy to see how you clasped your hands in prayer, Miss MacLeod."

"Thank you, Pastor Troyer."

"In the true Yoder Amish way."

"Thank you."

"So." Pastor Ropp, one of the old ministers that had served for over twenty years, leaned forward on the table that separated Kirsten from the men. "Tell us what else you know about the Yoder Amish. For instance, what do you have to say about a young woman's clothing when she is one of us, hm?"

Kirsten responded with the information she had gleaned from her reading, as well as what the Yoder Amish women had told her. Pastor Ropp nodded, asked about the threefold amen, nodded at her response to that as well, and sat back. Immediately, Pastor Graber, the other new pastor in addition to Pastor Troyer, began to pepper her with questions. His had more to do with the Bible, with what she believed about Jesus Christ, and how important her Christian faith was to her. Ropp interjected further questions about Bible reading, prayer, worship, and hymns, and if all these things were significant so far as her non-Amish lifestyle were concerned. Bishop Yoder finally weighed in with questions about a woman's role in the church and her role, in general, as a member of the Yoder Amish faith.

To lighten things up a bit, Pastor Troyer suddenly rapped loudly three times on the top of the large wooden table, grinning. "And what is that, Miss MacLeod?"

She smiled. "Someone is knocking at my door. Three times. It is the Yoder Amish way. It says the person paying me a visit is a believer in the Trinity."

"And what is the Trinity, Miss MacLeod?"

"The Trinity is God, Pastor Troyer, who manifests himself to us in three different ways; Father, Son, and Holy Spirit."

Pastor Graber spoke up: "How would you explain the Trinity to one of our children in a way they could understand, hm?"

She hesitated a moment before she replied. "So, I might ask them if they knew who Pastor Ropp was. The child would say yes. I would remind the boy or girl that he is one of our leaders and that sometimes he is wearing the hat of a Yoder Amish pastor. But I would also remind them he is a farmer and that he grows lots of barley and canola. Aren't his fields as yellow as the sun once July comes? Then brown with barley in the fall? So, then, sometimes Pastor Ropp wears the hat of a farmer. It is a different role than his calling as one of our ministers. He is still Pastor Ropp, but Farmer Ropp shows us a different part of himself. Farmer Ropp will talk about sun, and rain, and crops, and harvest, and how much he is able to sell his canola or barley for. Still Pastor Ropp, yes, but Farmer Ropp is a different part of Pastor Ropp. Then, I would remind them that he is a grandfather to friends of theirs: Deborah Ropp, Peter Ropp, and James Ropp. So, Grandfather Ropp plays hide and seek with them, he has candy in his pockets, he will carry them on his shoulders and pretend he is a horse –"

Pastor Ropp barked out a laugh.

"He does not carry the other pastors on his shoulders and pretend he is a horse when he has a meeting with them."

Ropp barked out another laugh.

"And he does not play hide and seek with the men who come to him to buy his crop of canola."

Pastor Troyer grinned. "*Ja*, that is for sure," and Bishop Yoder and all the ministers laughed –

even, Kirsten noted, a very dour Pastor Gore, who up until then had not made a sound.

"So," Kirsten concluded, "I would say to a child that just as Pastor Ropp wears three different hats, and we can experience Pastor Ropp in three different ways – pastor, farmer, and grandfather – yet he is still very much Pastor Ropp – so our God is always God, but sometimes he comes to us as a loving Father, sometimes as our Savior the Lord Jesus Christ with a very human face, and sometimes as the Holy Spirit, invisible to our eyes – just as the wind is – but moving on our hearts, and bringing us peace, and opening our eyes to understand things in the Bible we never noticed before."

Pastor Troyer nodded: "Such an answer is a blessing. *Danke*."

Pastor Ropp nodded as well. "*Gut*. It is *gut*."

Pastor Graber smiled. "It is well."

Bishop Yoder also smiled. Then he poured water from a pitcher into a tall glass. "Thank you for that explanation, my dear. Would you like a drink before we carry on?"

"*Danke*, Bishop Yoder. I would."

After she had placed her glass down, half-empty, Pastor Gore finally spoke up: "All this is fine. Your responses to the pastors are well put, and balanced, and true. We have noticed how you comport yourself in the worship services, at the Sunday lunches, at the hymn sings, *ja*, we have seen how you dress and act in public as well, and we are pleased. When you are with young Joshua Miller – your beau, huh? – your conduct has been exemplary, and a credit to your Christian faith, and it reflects well on the Yoder Amish you are increasingly identified with in Lancaster. We find no fault with anything you say or do and we can see how warmly you are embracing our faith a bit more every day. So, but my problem – our problem – is the same problem we had back in April, Miss MacLeod. Your family legacy. Your father, your brother, your fiancé – all soldiers. And you will not thrust that legacy aside. You will not disown or separate yourself from what they have done – the shedding of the blood of their fellow man. You know very well this is not the Amish way, yet here you sit in an effort to become one with us again, in an effort to be a woman of the Amish faith. But, before the face of the Lord, how can you join us? You will not repent of what your father, and brother, and fiancé have done – may they rest in peace, God willing. You even encouraged some of our people to attend the funeral of your late fiancé, Ty Samson, a Marine who had fought in Afghanistan, as well as a patriotic memorial to him only weeks ago. Shame. How can you lead our people astray so blatantly, when you know how the Yoder Amish feel about war and those who wage it?"

Kirsten bit her tongue, counted to fifteen as she met the hard gaze of a man as skinny as one of her split ends, and then responded, as she had rehearsed responding, to this sort of challenge from him. "With all due respect, Pastor Gore, I know you have spoken with the Amish families who attended the funeral procession for my fiancé, Sergeant Ty

Samson, as well for the memorial that took place at his graveside. So, you will know I did not ask or encourage any Amish families to attend either of those two events. I was as surprised as anyone to see them standing at the curbside and praying as Ty's casket was driven past. I was just as surprised to see the Amish work with Lance Corporal Brandon Peters to organize a memorial at Ty's gravesite where they sang hymns in German and prayed in German. There were no flags, no rifle volleys, and only Corporal Peters and the Protestant chaplain wore uniforms. God and country were not mentioned. Only God. God and Ty Samson. I had nothing to do with making the memorial a reality. But I attended. And I was blessed. I felt the touch of God in that cemetery and I was greatly blessed."

Pastor Gore was about to reply when Pastor Troyer interjected. "Do you yourself have any desire to join the military, Miss MacLeod?"

"No, sir, I do not."

"Do you have any wish to engage in warfare or to bear arms on behalf of your country?"

"No, sir." She took a deep breath. "But I do not despise those who do and who sacrifice their lives. Instead, I pray for their souls. And I pray for the grieving family members they have left behind. It seems to me this is what our Lord Jesus would have us do as Christian men and women."

Pastors Graber and Troyer both nodded.

Pastor Ropp folded his arms across his chest.

Pastor Gore shook his head and leaned across the table. "And how can you say what you have done is what our Lord Jesus Christ would have us do? How can you justify your actions by putting our Lord in your shoes and telling us he would say and do exactly the same things?"

"Because of what he told his disciples."

"And what did he tell his disciples?"

"*This is my commandment*," Kirsten recited from memory. "*That ye love one another, as I have loved you. Greater love hath no man than this, that a man lay down his life for his friends. Ye are my friends, if ye do whatsoever I command you.*" She paused. "Ty Samson laid down his life for his friends. Including you, Pastor Gore. He always considered the Amish of Lancaster County his friends. He always said he would do whatever he could to ensure that you would always be free to worship, and pray, and practice your faith in peace. Even if he had to die. Even if he had to lay down his life for his friends. Yes, even if he had to do what our Lord Jesus said." Kirsten struggled with the tears that stung her eyes, but she kept her eyes fixed on Pastor Gore. "*Greater love hath no man than this, that a man lay down his life for his friends.* Ty honored the words of the Lord Jesus, Pastor Gore. And so, we honored him. We did not honor war or killing. We honored the Lord Jesus and the young man who obeyed his commandment, to love as much as Jesus loved, even to the point of sacrificing his own life."

For several long moments, there was complete silence.

Pastor Troyer stood. "I call for the vote."

Bishop Yoder, struggling to control his own emotions, lifted a hand in admonition. "Pastor Troyer."

"We have seen enough of this young woman's soul. We know hers better than we know our own. If my brothers are in agreement, I call for the vote."

"Very well." Bishop Yoder looked at the pastors. "Shall we vote now, brothers? Shall we vote?"

"After five or ten minutes of silent prayer." Pastor Gore was staring at Kirsten, though his eyes were no longer as hard as they had been a half hour before. "It is our way."

Bishop Yoder nodded. "It is. I call for ten minutes of silent prayer and then the vote. Pastor Troyer, you may sit."

"I shall stand in this young woman's presence."

"As you wish."

They all bowed their heads. Kirsten felt the hotness of the tears on her cheeks, and was angry with herself, nor could she seem to find the right words to pray with, so she let the tears fall, and she let the pain in her heart and body be her prayer. The ten minutes seemed like an hour. Her mind remained absolutely blank. Finally, Bishop Yoder spoke up.

"Amen, amen, amen. Before God, we shall have the vote. Will you permit Kirsten MacLeod to take her vows and be baptized into the faith of the Yoder Amish? For my part, as your bishop, I shall permit." He rose to his feet. "*Ja*, I shall permit. Pastor Ropp?"

Pastor Ropp stood as Pastor Troyer and Bishop Yoder stood. "I shall permit."

"Pastor Troyer?"

"I shall permit."

"Pastor Graber?"

Pastor Graber got to his feet. "I shall permit."

"Pastor Gore?"

Pastor Gore did not respond and did not stir. His eyes were still closed.

"Pastor Gore?" the bishop asked a second time.

Pastor Gore remained seated with his eyes closed. Finally, he shook his head.

"There is too much at stake," he said quietly. "I know where this young woman's heart is. I know where she stands before God and how she would bless our church. But there is too much at stake. We cannot have anything to do with war or soldiers or uniforms. Even from a distance. Even without violence. Even when the heart seems so right and pure. Even when there is much love present and much faith. We cannot weaken our stance under any circumstances." Eyes still shut, he shook his head a second time. "I shall not stand. And I shall not permit. Before God and his Son, Jesus Christ, I shall not permit."

Bishop Yoder cleared his throat. "The vote must be unanimous. It is our way. I am sorry, Miss MacLeod. We must have consensus. It is the way of the Yoder Amish."

She got up. Her eyes were blurred by her tears. She bowed her head. She thanked them. She sensed that all of them wished to say something more to her, even Pastor Gore, but she told them she could not stay, and she fled the room, running out the front door past a startled Mrs. Yoder, stumbling down the steps of the porch to her pickup, almost flooding the engine again, jerkily backing up, and lurching forward, and racing down the road, too fast, she knew that, far too fast, and far too disrespectful for an Amish neighborhood.

Kirsten did not go home. She made her way to the riverside, where she and Josh had so happily declared their love for one another, and there she parked, and there she watched the river stream past like a golden torrent in the setting sun, and there she cried herself dry. Once the sun had vanished, she reached for a blanket folded up in the back of the cab, tugged it around herself, and fell asleep behind the wheel. She did not wake in time for work, and when the sunlight finally pierced her eyelids at ten in the morning, having finally cleared the tops of the trees close to the truck, she correctly judged the time from where the sun stood in the August sky, and she did not care.

At ten-thirty, she called Zook's Diner to apologize, and said she was sick to her stomach, which was true. Cook did not give her a hard time. She climbed out of the pickup, blanket still around her shoulders, and walked to the river bank. There had been several huge thunderstorms that week. The rain had swollen the creeks and streams that fed the river, and it moved along more quickly than usual, and was big, and fat, and full to the brim. Her heart, on the other hand, felt just the opposite.

They would never call her in for another interview. She knew that. Only the dissenter or dissenters could make that call. And it was not in Pastor Gore to do that. It would never happen.

Never. Not, she realized, because Pastor Gore hated her. In fact, she doubted that he even disliked her. But because his stance was so utterly different from her stance – he could not see her point of view and he did not wish to see her point of view. It was intolerable to him and had no place in his faith or his religion. It was something that simply could not be. And it was something his God could not be. Therefore, it was also something Kirsten Macleod could not be nor could she be allowed to bring that spirit and belief into the Yoder Amish. Never and never, amen.

"So, what do I do now, Lord?" she whispered, watching the sun flash off the water so vividly it seemed like the current was full of gems. "Keep on butting my head against a brick Amish wall? Or move on? I think, you know, it must be that I move on."

She closed her eyes, the breeze unraveling her hair from the tight bun she had created the evening before, so that it fell over her shoulders, over her face and eyes, over her blanket, and even over her arms and hands.

"I have to go, Josh," she said in a soft voice. "I'm not sure where yet, but I'll only have peace once I begin to pack my bags, and fill cardboard boxes with my socks, and my bling jeans, and my cowboy boots. I shall not take my ankle-length dresses, or my black shoes, and, in time, I shall forget how to pray with my hands clasped one over the other and inverted. For I am not meant to be Amish, Josh. Not Yoder Amish, not Beachy Amish, not any kind of Amish. It's just not what God wants for me.

"So, I am leaving Amish country and getting as far away from it as I can. And you know what the hardest thing is? I can't take you with me. I love you more than I love my own breath, but I can't take you with me. You and I are on two different planets. I think I'm still on Neptune while you're shoeing your Percherons on Earth. I have to go, you have to stay, and there's nothing either of us can do about it. I'll marry someone else, I'll have someone else's children, and you'll marry Sarah Fisher – she's pretty – or Ruth Troyer – she's even prettier, and so clever, and her father, Pastor Troyer, is a wonderful, warm-hearted man, perfect for taking on the role of a young blacksmith's father-in-law. We shall have the lives that God wills. It's just . . . it's just that we weren't God's will. And that hurts. Often enough, God's ways hurt, even if they are for the best. And this, well, this, is just like the rock song I was supposed to forget about and leave behind in my crazy *Englisch* world – this cuts like a knife, my Lord, oh, my God, this cuts like a knife."

Chapter 14

Kirsten knew that Josh would go to her house looking for her, to the diner, to their favorite haunts like the pond or the riverside, but she wasn't ready to talk to him, not about what she knew she had to say, so she drove out of Lancaster and nursed a coffee at a small truck stop, and let an hour or two go by. She felt terrible about doing that to him, she could only imagine how anxious or upset he must be, but she had to collect her thoughts, rehearse what she was going to say – it seemed like she was always rehearsing something she needed to say to the Amish – and rein in her emotions. She had no intention of bursting into tears with him or doing anymore crying than she has already done in private. Tears weren't going to fix a thing with Josh any more than they had fixed a thing with the bishop and the pastors. She and the Amish were over. She and the Amish farrier were over. It had to be said, it had to be said quickly, and then she had to get out of Dodge. She had already called the real estate agent who claimed she had a long list of prospective buyers for Kirsten's family home.

She asked the waitress to pour a fifth cup. Noon became one and one became two. Regardless of how frantic Josh might be to locater her, he had a job to do, and he had a work ethic. Plows had been damaged. Buggy wheels broken. Horses needed to have their hooves trimmed, and cleaned, and fresh shoes put in place. She knew Josh would not let the people down who came to him for help. He might spend a couple of hours hunting for her, but no more. Then he'd have to be back at his forge.

"I won't do anything to myself, you know that," she whispered across the table to a Joshua who wasn't there. "You don't ever have to worry that I would be so desperate as to attempt that. But you're right to think I'm about to pull a game changer. It's going to hurt us both. Badly. But we're survivors. In the end, we'll be okay."

At three, buzzed on more caffeine than she'd ever downed in her life, Kirsten drove back to Lancaster and the Miller home. She could see the smoke from the forge while she was till a block away. She parked and went around to the back of the house. She was still in the same Amish outfit she had worn to her interview the evening before. She had even fixed up her hair and tightened it into a bun again. Quietly, slowly, she took her place in front of the flames and sparks.

Josh did not see her for several minutes. He was bent over and hammering on the anvil, and working the bellows, goggles over his eyes, wearing a thick black leather apron that hung down past his knees, totally absorbed in his task. Kirsten did not move, did not fidget, did not speak. She watched him work through the smoke and flames. As she had watched him work a hundred times before. Only now it was different, so very different, because she loved him with all her heart, no holds barred, she had stopped being an innocent bystander months ago. He was everything a man should be to a woman and she ached for him even as she stood only fifteen or twenty feet away. How was it possible that she was going to lose him when she had only just found him?

If feelings could bleed, she thought to herself as a hammer blow sent up a shower of red sparks, *I'd be standing in a puddle of my own blood.*

"Kirsten." He had lifted his head and seen her. For a moment, he did not move. "Thank God, Kirsten. You are all right." Then he ripped off his goggles and apron and ran to her, crushing her in his arms and burying his face in her neck and hair. "Thank God, thank God, thank God."

She clung to him, smelling the fire and steel of the forge on his clothes, and cried helplessly. This had not been what she rehearsed. This had not been how she'd wanted things to go. They weren't supposed to touch at all, there was going to be no tears, she was to have stayed twenty or thirty feet away from him, and never touched him, and told him her piece, after which she was to have walked nobly, and stoically, and tragically away. That was going to be the extent of the drama. Now she could hardly get her words out and she felt like she could never let go of him, not if a hundred Percherons, with all their strength, tried to drag her out of his arms.

"I'm sorry, I'm sorry," she sobbed, choking on her words. "They said no, they said no again . . ."

"All right, it's all right, that doesn't change how I feel about you, Kirsten. We'll try again."

"No . . . no . . . we aren't going to try again. Pastor Gore would have to request that and . . . that is something he is never going to do . . . you know that."

"People change. God knows people change. He changes them."

"Not that man, he doesn't. Pastor Gore thinks God and himself are joined at the hip." She hugged Josh as hard as she could. "I have to leave, my handsome Amish farrier. I have to leave, my love. I do."

"Leave? Leave where? You just got here."

"I have to leave Lancaster. I have to leave Pennsylvania. I have to leave the Amish as far behind as I possibly can. And that means you too."

"No, no, don't be rash, you can't just run because the leadership have turned you down."

"I'm not . . . I'm not running. But I guess I feel like I am escaping. I have to find a place where I can breathe. I have to go somewhere that Kirsten MacLeod is welcomed and valued and . . . and . . . cherished."

"But I . . . I cherish you. You know I do. Before God and his Son, you must know I do."

She pulled back and smiled at him, her eyes wet and glistening. "You are not supposed to be making oaths, my Amish man." She kissed him on the lips. "Yes, of course I know how you feel about me. Of course, I know that you treasure me. I am your *Englisch* princess. But the Yoder Amish do not share your feelings."

"I heard that all the others voted for you."

"They did."

"Even the bishop."

"Yes."

"So, how can you say no one values you, or wants you, or cares about you? Many people adore you. Not just I. Many, many want you to be part of our faith and our church. Just watch. In a week, two weeks, a month, before Christmas, Pastor Gore will change his mind. He'll have to. The influence of the others will be too great. He will have to pray about it. Reconsider. God will soften his heart."

"Or he will reject all counsel."

"He . . ."

"He is a stubborn man. Well, I can be stubborn too. I have tried twice. I have laid bare my heart and my soul before your bishop and your pastors. It has gotten me nowhere. And it makes me sad. And bitter. I don't want to be sad and bitter. I don't want to see Pastor Gore at the diner, or at Schlabach's Meats, and have to smile at him as if everything is okay. It's not okay. He hasn't just separated me from the Amish faith. He's separated me from you."

"No. No, he hasn't."

"Of course, he has. We can't be together. You can't keep on courting a woman who will never become Amish and I can't keep dating a man I love, but who I can never marry. It's not going to work anymore. This isn't a buggy ride in a thunderstorm. It's just the storm and it's a storm that isn't going away. It's killing me, oh, it's killing me, but I have to let go of you completely – you, Lancaster, the Yoder Amish, all my wishes and dreams, I have to walk away and start again. My house . . . my house is already being listed."

His eyes looked as if she had struck him physical blows. She cringed at the sight, but there was no going back. She had not created this nightmare, but she had to get out of it, they both had to get out of it, and the only way she could see herself clear of all the pain, and disappointment, and heartbreak was to get out of the county, get out of the state, move to Colorado, move to Florida, and do a reset, have a fresh start, with none of her past life nearby, nothing of what she was on the verge of saying goodbye to clinging to her, and holding her back, or holding her down.

"You have to see this for what it is, Josh," she begged, watching the hurt in his eyes grow. "What else can we possibly do? I am not going to be Amish. Not ever. You are never going to have me as an Amish wife. The dream is over. Dead. *Kaput.* As hard as it is, we have to steel ourselves, face the reality, deal with the inevitable, and move on. Our old wishes and dreams don't matter anymore, Josh. We have to find new ones. I do and you do. My love, my love, don't think I don't feel like someone is carving the heart out of my chest. I'm dying. I'm bleeding and dying. This is way too much drama for this Pennsylvania girl. I need a curtain on it. I need an ending. Quickly. Before I bleed to death, and can't do anything, but curl up in a ball in my den and cry for the next twenty years. I can't do a forever pity party, Josh, I can't. I have to let you go, you have to let me go, and we have to walk away from each other, and try again with somebody else. We both have to do it. There isn't any other choice."

His mouth suddenly covered hers, and she could feel all his pain, and love, and hurt, and desperation pouring into his kiss. He held her more and more tightly, as if he could keep her from leaving and stop what was ripping them apart from happening. She responded with a stronger hug than she had ever given him, ever given anyone, and put all of herself into the kiss, knowing it could be their last, knowing if she had the courage to follow through on her plans to leave Lancaster as fast as she possibly could, that it *would* be their last.

It is the best way, Josh, the only way that will work for us, the only way that will cause as little pain as possible. If we prolong the goodbye, if I hang out in Lancaster another two or three months, how will that help you or me? The hurt will never end if I do that. At least, once I am out of Pennsylvania, even though it will still be some of the worst pain you or I have ever experienced, it won't last long, it can't last long, because I'll be really gone, and you'll move on, and I'll move on, and in time, we won't suffer as much anymore, we just won't, because we'll have new lives. But I'll never forget you.

She pulled her lips from his. "I'll never stop thinking about you, Josh. You have to know that. Never. I wish it had worked out. Oh, the Lord knows how I prayed it would work out. But his ways are not our ways and his plans are not our plans. He doesn't think like us and we never see the whole picture like he does. All we can do is pray for God's best, expect to receive it, and then work with what we've got. And my leaving is what we've got. You are meant to marry an Amish woman and raise a family with her. And I am meant to marry a good Christian man who is not Amish and raise a family with him. That's what's meant to be, Josh. It's what's meant to be."

He gripped her arms with his large hands. "I have not stopped praying yet. I have not stopped hoping yet. I haven't stopped anything to do with you or me yet. And I pray you haven't either."

Kirsten drank in his intense blue eyes a few moments, loving the sweet sensation they always gave her, taking some happiness from the fact that he was still hers, and so badly wanted to stay hers, and would stay hers for months, maybe years after she had left Lancaster County. Then she closed her eyes and shook her head. No, no, she did not want him pining away at his forge, hoping she'd change her mind and come back to him. She wanted him to find someone else. She did not want him to keep on suffering. Placing her hands on his chest, she pushed him back.

"You have to let me go," she insisted, and just saying those words made tears cut down her cheeks again. "We have to let each other go. I need to be gone in a week, Josh. Even if my house hasn't sold, I am getting on the freeway and heading south in seven days."

"If God wills."

"He already has willed."

"You don't know that."

"Of course, I know it. You know it too. You just won't accept it."

"I'll never accept it."

"You'll have to. You'll just have to. We'll both have to. Or we'll never get through this."

He seized her once again and kissed her as if he were a fire. *Like the fire in his forge*, she thought, as the power of his love swept through her body. Just like the flames at her back that she could feel from twenty or thirty feet away. And whenever a gust managed to reach the smithy, she felt the flames even more as they leaped up and devoured the air.

She felt engulfed by both Josh and his forge. She felt like she was being burned alive. One fire was no less potent or intense than the other. His arms pinned her to him, and she could not wriggle loose, so she gave in and let him be her inferno. It was like experiencing some kind of flashover, going from intense conversation one moment, and in another moment, in a sudden kiss, erupting into heat and flames, and both of them overcome, and both of them not going anywhere except up in flames and ash, both powerless to put out even the smallest spark, as their love for each other turned them into pillars of yellow, and red, and orange. She had daydreamed about melting him with her kisses. Now the two them melted together, and fused, and for the ten or fifteen minutes the fiery kisses lasted, became one. Then somehow, impossibly, for her strength was gone, she tore herself away from him, and ran from the smithy.

"Kirsten." He stood watching her go. "Kirsten."

Against her better judgment, she glanced back at him, saw his devastation, realized she shared it, and began to crack apart inside all over again.

"We can't keep going like this, Josh." She called back. "We can't. It's not something humans can endure. Goodbye is goodbye is goodbye and that's what I'm saying to you."

"I cannot believe God is finished with us yet. I cannot."

"Don't come to my house, Josh. Please. Don't show up for my last shifts at the diner. Don't ride up to my door with your buggy thinking you can save this, that you can save us. We can't say goodbye a hundred times and think that will make it any easier. Just know that I love you, just know that I love you so much I can't catch my breath when I think about leaving you. That has to be enough. Knowing how huge my love is. Goodbye at this forge is goodbye forever. I never want to see you again, my love. Never. I can't. I swear to God, my big, beautiful man, I can't."

Chapter 15

"I saw you at the 9/11 memorial this morning. Far at the back."

Josh looked up from a broken harness he was examining.

Brandon Peters was standing in front of him in dress blues.

"Corporal Peters," Josh said.

"Blacksmith Miller," Brandon replied.

Josh offered a small smile and nodded. "*Ja.* I saw you too."

"If you saw me too then you saw who was with me."

Josh nodded again. "*Ja.*"

"I was her escort. Nothing more. It's over between us. Well over."

Josh shrugged with one shoulder. "*Ja.* Well. It is well over between her and I as well. So, it doesn't matter to me who she attends 9/11 memorials with."

"No?"

"*Nein.* I have had almost a week to think it over, haven't I? So, she has made her decision. And, *ja*, it's true, others have made decisions for her as well. And she is going, no matter what I say or do. Is there anything you can tell her, Corporal, that will make her change her mind about your relationship? Of course not. She is going to go off and live her life without you. And now she is going to go off and live her life without me too. She will have her happily ever after with someone else. You appear to have accepted it and moved on. So must I."

"Do you assume she is happy or something, Blacksmith Miller?"

"I honestly don't know what she is, Corporal Peters. I have not seen her since last Wednesday. She forbids me to go to her house. Forbids me to see her. Touch her. Hold her. She is in my head, that's all, only in my head. There is no reality. Just a memory. Sometimes I think I have forgotten exactly the way her face is. Or her smile. Or the way she tosses her hair – you know how she does that."

"I know."

"She is off limits to me. That is the way she wanted it and that is the way it is. I respect her and I respect her boundaries. Happy? I think she is happy about saying goodbye to Lancaster and being done with an Amish community whose leadership could never welcome her into the fold. Leaving her friends, her family home, you, me – okay, I know this cannot be easy for her. There is not going to be much happiness in her heart over doing that. But, you know, in life, we are always trading one thing for another. I am being traded off for Florida or Colorado. She is making a bargain with God for her freedom and a new life. She gives me up for someone else and for another place to live. So, I go back to my tools, and my forge, and my church without her."

Josh went back to examining the harness. He wanted to say something else to Brandon, hesitated, dismissed the thought, but then spoke the words out loud anyways: "Did you ever – forgive me, if I am saying too much, but the last week has been like, like, someone has been cutting me up with a butcher knife – did you ever imagine what it would be like to . . . to wake up with her sleeping beside you?"

"Many times."

"That she would be your wife and that she would be by your side for thirty or forty or fifty years?"

"Yes."

"And . . . still look as beautiful as the day you married her?"

Brandon smiled. "Yeah. I know the feeling."

"So, how did you let go of that? How?"

"I didn't. But I'm a Marine. You learn to live with pain and suffering. It comes with being a warrior. So yeah, I miss her. And yeah, I still daydream about her and being married to her. And yeah, it cuts like a Ka-Bar knife. But I suck it up. And I go forward."

Josh offered up another weak smile. "So, I will have to be an Amish Marine and do the same thing."

"Except you have one option open to you that was not open to me, Blacksmith Miller."

"And what is that, Corporal Peters?"

"She is miserable without you."

Josh did not respond. Inside, he felt surprise. And confusion.

"There are still things you can do and say that will change everything. Maybe not the minds of the men who run your church. But just about everything that has to do with you and her. And that's what counts." Brandon seemed to draw up his shoulders and place himself at attention. "Fight for her."

"*Vas?*"

"Refuse to take no for an answer. Refuse to surrender. Refuse to accept the limitations she's placed on you. Refuse to admit you can't attain your objective or fulfill your mission. Go after her."

"But she's said . . ."

"I don't care what she's said. What do you say? What does all the pain inside you say? Do you want her or not?"

"Of course, I want her. What man wouldn't want her?"

"Then get going, Marine, and win back her heart."

"I cannot go against her wishes."

"How do you know what her wishes are? How do you know what she said to you last Wednesday is what she's still thinking this Monday morning? How do you know she isn't waiting for you to come, and take her in your arms, and tell her you can't live or breathe or exist without her? That you'll do anything to keep her, anything." Brandon paused and his eyes became thin slits. "Are you ready to do anything?"

"I . . . "

"How far are you willing to go to win her back? You talked about a tradeoff. What are you willing to trade off to make her yours forever? How far are you willing to push it? How much does she matter to you?"

"Look, she was fine before I came into her life and she is more than fine now that I am out of it."

"Skip the "pity me". Just answer my questions. Is she the first thing in your life? Second? Third? How far are you willing to go to have her as your wife and to see her asleep in your bed next to you? What are you willing to give up?" Brandon lowered his voice. "Because you can still have what you want the most, Marine. You can. If she is what you want the most. You can have her in your arms before the sun sets. *If. If she really is what you want more than anything else in your life.*"

"There . . . there is God to consider . . . faith . . . a man's family . . ."

"Yes. Yes, there is." Brandon glanced at his watch. "You have twelve hours. Probably much less. She could be pulling out of Lancaster in half an hour if the moving van is ready to go. Good luck, God bless, and goodbye. Do what you have to do."

"I find all this difficult."

"So does she. But at the crack of dawn or sooner she is definitely gone. If you want her at your side until the day you die, fight for her."

Brandon marched away from the forge. Josh heard his truck start and the gravel pop under its tires. His head was reeling. He leaned forward and rested the weight of his body on his hands. Nothing was clear. Nothing was obvious. He liked things to be simple and straightforward. And solid. He had a hard time with thoughts, and ideas, and feelings he couldn't pin down. Kirsten whirled and spun in his head.

Who was she? Who was she supposed to be? And he himself – who and what was he when he placed himself beside her? Was he less? More? Better? Worse? Closer to God? Farther? What kind of a man was he when she was around? What did she bring out of him? How strong did she make his world, how solid did she make his faith, how much did she matter, truly matter?

Can you honestly let her go?

Before God, can she never be part of your life ever again?

Never?

Josh broke for the stables. He had no time for a buggy or cart. Gretchen had been ridden bareback and with a saddle. But Josh did not have time for the saddle either. He slipped the bit between the mare's teeth, tossed the reins up over her neck, sprang on her back, and spoke rapidly to her in German. She moved quickly out of the stables, and across the yard, and onto the road. A buggy was snapping along in front of them, and another pulled in behind them, and Josh stayed between the two for several miles while cars and pickups whizzed past. But his blood was up, and the mare sensed it, so her blood was up too, and soon the buggy in front was a hindrance, not a help.

So, Josh and Gretchen peeled out past it, and its startled driver, Peter Beiler, the Yoder Amish bootmaker, and with a wave, Josh and his shining black mare began to gallop in the ditch at the side of the roadway. Faster and faster, Josh urged his horse on, her hooves kicking up grass and mud. Taking a back road, Josh avoided traffic and did not let up on the mare, using German words to coax her to keep up her swift pace, until he raced out onto Kirsten's street, and took in the large moving van, and the furniture laid out on her lawn, and the dozens of cardboard boxes. He jumped off Gretchen, in front of a couple of men who were struggling with a grandfather clock, almost making them drop it, checked to be sure Kirsten's Chevy was still at the curb, tied his mare to a small bush, and went through the front door, pretty much running down a man and a woman who were wrestling with a brown piano. Kirsten was in the center of the living room, surrounded by even more boxes and stacks of furniture, explaining something to a hefty man with a red beard. She was dressed in jeans, cowboy boots, a baggy T-shirt, and had her hair in a ponytail, and when she turned her head, and saw Josh, the blood ran out of her face instantly, so that she was as white as the high summer clouds outside the door.

"Don't say anything," Josh begged. "Don't say a word. Let me speak these things that are fresh in my head."

Kirsten stared at him, but did not move or open her mouth.

"God is everywhere. We believe that, *ja*? He is in India or China at the same time he is in America or Lancaster County. So, he is not just the God of the Amish, but the God of everyone. Before this God, I love the Amish, I love the Amish ways, I love the slow pace, the gentleness, the quiet, the tools I use with my own strength and not electricity, I love our prayers, I love our worship. But I love you more. I love the Amish, and I love my family, but Kirsten MacLeod, before God, I love you more."

Kirsten's eyes were as large as moons, but still she did not respond. The packers had stopped their work to watch.

"If I cannot be Amish, I can still be a farrier and a blacksmith. If I cannot be Amish, I can still worship God in my house, at my forge, in my barn, in another church. If I am not in Lancaster, I can still be Joshua Miler, and raise a family, and make a living with my two hands, and bring bread to the table, and say grace with my hands clasped. What I cannot do . . . what I can never do . . . is live my life without Kirsten MacLeod. It is impossible to be the man I am supposed to be without you. I can never do the work I ought to do without your presence. I cannot do anything that matters in this world, anything, without your love. I must have your love. I'm dead without it. I have no future, and no hope, and no desire. I am lost and confused. I'm a wagon wreck. But with you and your love, everything makes sense. Everything becomes clear. The whole of God's world, and all that is in it, takes on its proper size, and proportions, and its splendor. This sounds so much. It sounds too much. Too much for me to say. But it's true. Your love is everything. You are everything. I am miserable without you."

Josh dropped to one knee.

"Marry me, Kirsten MacLeod," he said. "We don't have to be Amish. We just have to be us. Marry me, Kirsten MacLeod. And put me out of my misery."

Chapter 16

September
Monday, Kirsten's house, 12 noon

Kirsten felt like the world had been yanked out from under her feet.

One minute she had been discussing which storage unit her household goods were being sent to at a facility in Lancaster.

In her mind, she had forced Joshua Miller far, far away. Her only reality was packing, and moving, and shedding tears over leaving her family home, and thinking of how many miles she would put between her and Lancaster before she stopped for the night. She knew that eventually Josh would force his way back into her thoughts – he had never left her heart – but he was not something she wanted to deal with amidst the turmoil of the biggest change she had ever made in her life. She had placed him in a safe place in her head, and locked him in there as tightly as she could, and turned the key.

At no time had Kirsten ever believed Josh would violate her request that he stay away from her. Good Amish boys didn't do things like that. She hadn't expected to ever see him again. She had cried over him every day since she had fled from his forge, but she was convinced she was making the right decision. They were over. And they were over because she and the Amish were over. So over. There was nothing more to say or do when it came to the Yoder Amish. As far as she was concerned, breaking with them meant breaking with Josh, because he would never leave them.

"Kirsten."

He was on one knee in front of her, for heaven's sakes. Boxes and furniture all around. Packers and movers staring. Time frozen. She had signed off on the house, and the sale was contingent on the buyers selling their own home, which was supposed to go through at any minute. Everything was set. But now this. Now this.

"Kirsten. *Ich liebe dich. Ich liebe dich fur immer.*"

I love you forever.

Oh Lord God in heaven, she prayed, what do you want me to do?

You are not supposed to be here, Josh Miller. You are not supposed to be at my house. You are not supposed to be disrupting my plans. You are not supposed to be proposing to me. You are not supposed to be breaking the rules and saying you'll leave the Yoder Amish for me. You are not supposed to put me on the spot like this. You can't do this. You can't.

His eyes were too blue. Too big. Too sincere. Too full of passion. She told herself to look away, but couldn't. She ordered herself to walk away, but she couldn't do that either. His effect on her was hypnotic. She was determined to break the spell: *Just close your eyes, just close your eyes for one minute, and when you open them again, poof, he will be gone.*

"Kirsten. Nothing else matters. God is in his heaven, and nothing else is as important as you. Nothing. Kirsten, *Du bist die Liebe meines Lebens.*"

She had made a lot of progress with her German, but this phrase was new to her. Yet her mind quickly connected the dots. You . . . love . . . life . . . mine . . .

"Du bist die Liebe meines Lebens, Kirsten."

You are the love of my life.

"Oh, Josh!"

Everything inside her exploded.

"Josh Miller!"

Tears were racing down her cheeks and she'd sworn there would be no more tears over him, no more, never, enough.

"I love you, I love you." Kirsten hurled himself into his arms and they both collapsed onto the floor in a tangle of arms and legs. She kissed his face and lips over and over again. He wrapped his arms around her.

"My lunky Amish blacksmith," she cried. "Yes, yes, YES."

The packers began to clap, and whistle, and Kirsten went from crying to laughter, and could not stop.

"This is crazy," she said, continuing to pepper Josh with her kisses. "You're crazy. Everything's crazy. None of this was supposed to happen. Not ever. Not like this. Not now. Nothing makes sense. Nothing."

"I love you makes sense," he responded, burying his face in her hair.

"That's the only thing that does make sense. I love you and you love me. Everything else is insane."

"So, let's enjoy the love."

"Oh, yes, we can enjoy the love. But then what? What comes after your marriage proposal on my moving day?"

"The marriage, of course."

"Just like that?"

"Sure." He snapped his fingers. "Are you ready?"

She laughed. "Oh, I'm ready, all right. Do you mind if I change into something more comfortable though? Something white?"

"I'll wait."

"Good. Because it could take an hour or two."

"Not a problem. But you are perfectly beautiful as you are."

"*Danke schoen.* But part of this girl's fantasy did not include getting married in blue jeans and a pair of cowboy boots. She did have something with a bit more dazzle in mind."

"I look forward to it."

"And are we going to tell anyone?" Kirsten asked. "Or is this a kind of Amish elopement?"

"We will tell my mother and father," Josh said.

"Fun. I like them."

"And we will tell Bishop Yoder as well."

"Even more fun. I like him too."

"And he will tell Pastor Gore."

"And then the fun stops."

Josh laughed and patted her on the back. "That is when the true fun begins. You will see."

"My, my, don't you sound confident."

"You said yes." He laughed again. "You said yes. And it has made me delirious. I can't think straight for the first time in my life. Or maybe it is the second or third time. There were all the kisses you have given me, after all, and the way you toss your hair. But for sure, right now, at this moment, the Amish farrier cannot think straight."

"Good." She grinned. "I hope it stays that way. Because the thinking that has come out of you since we fell on the floor has been your best thinking yet."

September
Monday, the riverside, 3:17 PM

It took them a half hour to get out of the buggy after they parked because their kissing was non-stop.

When they sat together in the tall grass under the trees, grass so high no one could have seen them even if the person were standing ten feet away, the kissing continued, him murmuring to her in German, she murmuring to him in English, his lips on her hair, her eyebrows, her cheeks, her throat, her chin. She laughed at his energy.

"It's like you've never kissed me before or something," she giggled.

"I haven't," he responded. "Not as my fiancé."

"Well, don't forget the lips then, you amateur. They're more important than my chin."

"I love your chin."

"I thought you loved me."

"I love your chin and you."

"Do you love my eyes?" Kirsten teased.

"Your big brown eyes? Of course, I do."

"What about my arms?"

"I worship your arms."

"Worship them, do you? And my elbows? My feet?"

"Everything. I worship everything."

"Even when my feet are in those clunky black Amish shoes?"

"Especially then."

"Oh, this is so unlike us." Kirsten kissed Josh's chin. "There. I love yours too."

"What is unlike us? To be in love and acting like sixteen year olds?"

"No. We've acted like sixteen year olds plenty of times before. It's you going ahead and telling your parents you are marrying me, even if you must leave the Yoder Amish to do it. It's me putting a hold on the sale of my house. It's you saying to your bishop, *Thus and thus shall it be, if you will not permit us to be a married couple among the Yoder Amish, we shall be a married couple among the Beachy Amish or among the Amish in Ohio, or Michigan, or even Ontario, Canada, or far west among the Amish of*

Montana. And it's me saying to him, *No, mein Herr, I do not renounce my father or brother or fiancé for their military service. I do not need to renounce them to marry an Amish boy. Ach,* we are breaking all the rules. Since when have we broken all the rules?"

"Love does funny things to a person."

"Yeah? Well, I love being in love with you. And I love kissing you in the buggy and in this tall timothy. I even love the randomness of your showing up at my door when I told you not to – it's exciting. But I don't know how exciting it will be to talk to speak with Pastor Gore tonight, love or no love."

She noticed all her talking had not done anything to cool her Amish farrier's ardor. So, she went back to concentrating on kissing and embracing for a few minutes, then lay back in the grass and let him nuzzle her neck and shoulder while she twisted his hair into tight coils with her fingers.

"I'm not sure how excited I will be to face off with the ministers a third time tonight," she said, picking up where she'd left off.

His kisses on her skin were as warm and soft as summer raindrops. "You do not seem as anxious as you were before the meeting a week ago."

"I guess . . . I guess I'm not. Though I should be."

"Why should you be?"

"They can say no to the marriage."

"No. They can't. We get married here or we get married there. It doesn't matter if we are with the Amish of Pennsylvania or the Amish of Idaho. Or with no Amish at all. It makes no difference to me. And it shouldn't to you."

"I feel terrible taking you away from your people."

"But I want to be with you. I truly want to be with you. Let me be happy in your arms."

"You nut. Of course, I want you to be happy in my arms. I don't want you to be happy anywhere else."

"So, that is settled. And that's why you are not so anxious about tonight. Before, yes, they could stop you from joining the Yoder Amish. Tonight, no, they cannot stop us from loving each other or being wed. That is why you are not so worked up."

Kirsten thought about it. "Okay. Maybe."

He kissed her on the ear. "And maybe something else."

"Ohhh. That tickles." She laughed and pushed his head away. "What something else?"

"The other meetings, you were always alone. You won't be this time."

"No. I thank God."

"So . . ."

"Yes. Of course. You being there relaxes me. I feel like . . . like you will protect me. Will you?"

"As if you must ask me when you know very well what the answer is."

"Sometimes a woman just asks things to be sure she isn't dreaming."

"All right." Josh smiled. "So, you are wide awake. See how blue the sky is."

"How green the grass," she responded.

"How swift the river."

"How white the clouds."

"How loud the bees."

"How soft the breeze." She reached up with a long blade of timothy and stroked underneath his chin. "Everything is perfect. So, maybe I am dreaming after all."

"That would mean good things only happen in dreams, while reality only offers up pain and disappointment. Do you believe that?"

She smiled and continued to stroke him with the timothy. "Not really."

"And, after all, dreams can turn into nightmares."

"They can."

"While reality can become too good to be true and surprise us."

"It often does."

He lay beside her, propping himself up on one elbow, and smoothed her hair back from her forehead. "So, don't be anxious to any degree about the bishop or the pastors. The greatest is love, *ja*? That is what will win out."

"I am actually more concerned about your parents than our meeting with the leadership."

Josh shook his head slightly. "No need. You saw them. You heard them. They support us. They believe our marriage is of God."

"Still. They have to face the other Amish families. They have to face the bishop and pastors on Sunday mornings. Surely, some will look down on them because they have failed to raise their son well enough to keep him in the Amish faith."

"Ha. You think so?"

"I do."

"You are assuming we will be rejected by not only the Yoder Amish, but all the Amish communities and become like the *Englisch, ja*?"

She shrugged. "Maybe."

"Is that what you think when you pray?"

"I don't think anything when I pray. Not about this. My mind doesn't wander and neither do I have images or ideas about what I want to happen. It is just . . . just like a clear blue stream coming out of the hills, the very green hills. I feel God's presence, I feel his love, yes, I can honestly say I even feel his affirmation and support. But I don't have any answers from heaven either. Mind you, someone hasn't given me very much time to pray."

"Who? Me?"

"Who? You? Who else has been kissing me ever since lunchtime? And we didn't even have lunch."

"I don't need food."

"No?"

"No. I shall live on love and my forge."

She giggled. "What are you going to make on your forge? Hamburgers?"

"Why not? Charcoal broiled. I could also do chicken that way. And steak."

"And *Bratwurst*."

"Of course, always *Bratwurst*. But not to forget *Blutwurst*."

"Who forgot *Bratwurst*? I have developed a taste for it. So, I will live on love and *Blutwurst* and . . . prayer. Can we?"

"Of course, we can."

They both sat up. He put his arm around her shoulders and began to pray softly in German. She understood some of it. It did not matter to her if she understood all or even most of it. When he was silent, she prayed out loud in German too. Not very long and her prayers were not very complex. Then she murmured prayers in English too. After hers, he whispered German prayers once more.

She fell asleep leaning against him, woke up, fell asleep a second time, woke up to a crimson sky in the west and the sun half gone.

"Are we late?" she asked, snuggling.

"No. There's plenty of time."

"I'm getting chilled."

"We'll head back. And there are blankets in the buggy."

"I'm hungry too."

"I thought you were going to live on love," he teased.

"No. Love and *Blutwurst* and prayer. I've had the love and the prayer – though I wouldn't kind some more of both – but now I need the blood sausage, the *Blutwurst*."

"I know a place."

"A good place?"

"For sure. My mother's kitchen."

"They aren't expecting us," Kirsten protested.

Josh shrugged with one shoulder. "As if it matters. She always cooks enough for fifty."

He got up and helped her to her feet.

"You don't know that it will be *Blutwurst*," she argued.

"I do know. It's Monday. I know the menu for Monday. There will be cabbage, as well. Perhaps asparagus wrapped in Canadian bacon. Some sweet potato. Lemonade. And coffee."

"No dessert?"

"Pie, I think. Rhubarb."

"I love rhubarb. Are you sure rhubarb?"

"Pretty sure. But apple strudel will do just as well. Or blueberry cobbler."

He tucked a thick woolen blanket around her as she sat in the buggy. "There."

She smiled. "Perfect."

"Like you."

"You are stretching the truth, but thank you."

Josh flicked the reins. "It's not too much of a stretch."

"My hero in shining armor. Again, thank you, Sir Knight."

"*Bitte.*"

He took his time getting them back into Lancaster. The crimson in the west deepened and glowed. It reminded her of Josh's forge and sometimes the color blazed up like it did when he worked the bellows vigorously. She did not speak or turn her eyes way from the sunset as the horse clopped along. It got into her head that she could find an answer from God in the ruby and vermillion colors. Maybe he liked speaking through what he'd created as much as he liked speaking into her mind through a Bible verse. Josh left her alone to her thoughts and musings, only reaching out to take her cold hand in one of his.

"You are as warm as the fire in your smithy, Amish blacksmith," she said quietly, keeping her eyes on the western sky.

"Does it help?"

"*Ja*. It helps."

For a few miles, they turned directly into the blaze of red. She imagined it was their future. Was it a Yoder Amish future? A future with any sort of Amish in it at all? Any of the peace, and quiet, and slow, rhythmic movement of that faith, the slow, rhythmic movement of a walking horse? Or was the sunset a portent of a different sort of destiny? Where an Amish man and his *Englisch* wife made their way on their own, keeping a bit of Amish here, a bit of *Englisch* there? They were driving into their tomorrows led by Josh's dark black mare, Gretchen. In a few hours, Kirsten would know whether she would wear the Amish woman's prayer *kapp* or keep her head bare before God, and the southern winds, and the perfect crystal snowflakes of December.

Chapter 17

The meal at the Miller house had been an unusually somber affair. Picking up on the mood of the adults, the children were silent, and there was no laughter or teasing. Josh's father prayed a long time when they first sat at the table and then prayed again just before they all got up to leave. Their time together was short, no more than twenty minutes, and Mrs. Miller had not offered any dessert. Kirsten only lingered to put on one of Mrs. Miller's dresses, and a pair of her black shoes, a size too large. The Miller family said they needed to be somewhere else and left. Josh shrugged, and went a roundabout way to the bishop's house, as if to try and dispel some of the gloominess that had fastened on Kirsten and himself at dinner.

"How are you feeling?" Josh asked Kirsten.

"Do you want me to be honest?"

"That is what I want, yes."

"I felt better down by the river."

He smiled a small smile. "Me too."

She smiled back and took his free hand. "But it's also true it makes a great deal of difference knowing you are going into that house with me."

"God is going into the house with us too."

"Well, hopefully he is already there."

Josh nodded towards the sky. It had turned a deep indigo with a faint ribbon of scarlet at its western border. Kirsten thought it looked like a navy blue counterpane. With a bright applique that imitated shining points of light.

"The first stars," Josh said.

"I see them. Beautiful."

"Are you going to make a wish?"

"Yes. I think I will. God knows that my wishes are often enough my prayers."

"I suppose I know what your wish will be."

Kirsten kept her eyes on the evening sky. "Perhaps you do, perhaps you don't."

"Does wishing on a star help you?"

"Sometimes. It helps even more when I remind myself those stars are different colors – some golden, some white, some blue, some red – and that they are really suns. Bright, warm, blazing suns. That cheers me up."

"So, I hope they are cheering you up right now."

"Surprisingly, yes, they are. The wishing game doesn't always help. But it's helping me tonight."

That was the first surprise.

What she thought of as the blessing of the stars.

The second came as they rounded a corner and saw the bishop's large home. Five or six buggies were parked in front of it and a number of adults and children were milling together in the yard. Including Josh's family, and the Schrocks, the Reimers, the family of Peter Beiler the shoemaker, and another family Kirsten did not know well, the Bontragers. She put a small fist to her mouth.

"But what's this, Josh?" she asked.

"I don't know."

"Did your father tell you they were going to be here?"

"No."

When they pulled up, several children ran to the buggy ahead of their parents.

"We are praying for you," one boy announced.

"*Ja*," agreed another. "We have all been praying."

Rebecca had a huge smile on her young face, a face sprinkled with the cheerful freckles the summer had gifted her with. "We believe it is God's will that you two marry and be part of our church. We have told the bishop and pastors this as well."

Mr. Miller, in his dark coat and hat and beard, laughed at Becca's exuberance. "It is true. We have spoken with the leadership. Our words were given to them with great humility and respect. But it is our right, as Yoder Amish, to voice our concerns to our bishop and pastors, just as occurred at the Council of Jerusalem, which we read about in the Holy Bible in the Book of Acts.

So, the bishop is not chagrined by our presence here."

"You said nothing to me about this," Josh responded.

"You and Kirsten had enough on your mind."

"The bishop knows we come in peace, as is fitting," added Peter Beiler, appearing at Mr. Miller's side. "He knows we support your marriage and Miss Macleod's inclusion among us. But he also knows that, first and foremost, we pray for God's will to be done tonight. We believe it shall be."

Adam Schrock was there. He reached up and grasped Kirsten's hand. "It is almost too many trips to the dentist for you, my dear."

Kirsten responded with a short laugh. "Yes, sometimes it feels that way, Mr. Schrock."

"But I see God's calm on their features. Our ministers are bound to hear the hopes and prayers of their people, and are charged with taking those into account as they approach the Lord about you and young Joshua. I am optimistic about the outcome this evening. I sense the touch of God upon all."

Mr. Reimer, and Mr. Bontrager, and two other men that Kirsten had seen at worship services and hymn sings, but did not know, arrived at the buggy to stand with the others.

"We believe it is a holy night," acknowledged Mr. Reimer.

"And that God's will does indeed reside in the hearts of his people," added tall, slender, and white-bearded Mr. Bontrager. "Bishop Yoder sees this. He understands what is going on here. God is present."

"They cannot fail to grasp what the Almighty wishes," said a heavy-set man Kirsten did not have a name for. "It is written on the faces of his people. Even the heavens declare the glory of God tonight and the firmament displays his handiwork. So it is with the Yoder Amish at this hour."

Amen, amen, amen, murmured the men and women who had encircled the buggy. Even Rebecca spoke the threefold amen and bowed her head. *Out of the mouth of babes,* thought Kirsten, and a great warmth came into her heart. Many hands helped her down from her seat, and blessings were uttered as she made her way to the porch, and the front door, with Josh. They paused there a minute to look back at the people crowded at the foot of the porch steps. Then Josh rapped three times. The door was opened almost instantly by Mrs. Yoder. Her smile was large and real.

"Come in, please," she invited Kirsten and Josh. She also paused to look at the cluster of Yoder Amish in her front yard. "The Lord be with you all," she greeted them.

"And also with you," dozens of voices, young and old, replied.

Kirsten received her third surprise as she and Josh entered the room where the bishop and pastors were seated at a large table. The men rose, and took their hands, and welcomed them with smiles and, Kirsten thought, a strong show of grace. Even Pastor Gore's eyes were kind when he shook her hand and his face was crinkled with a certain amount of warmth that, little as it was, seemed to bring him closer to her heart.

"So, you have brought the Lord's army with you tonight," joked Bishop Yoder.

"It is a great surprise to us," replied Josh. "We knew nothing about it."

The bishop waved a hand in the air. "It is not a problem for us. Such is the way of the Yoder Amish from time to time. Unquestionably, the Lord has something to say to us through it."

The pastors all nodded.

After the prayer, Bishop Yoder folded his hands on the tabletop. "There is no need for any preamble. Miss MacLeod has been with us several times. None of us here questions her commitment to our Lord or even her sincere desire to follow him as one of the Yoder Amish. And now you wish to marry her, Joshua Miller, and that we understand as well, for she is a young woman of Christian grace and humility. It does disturb us that you would marry her against our wishes if you felt that was necessary. That you would join with another Amish community or no Amish community at all. Nevertheless, we are pleased that you wished to discuss this with us, and pray with us, and not run off and do whatever you wished. For that we commend you."

Pastor Ropp was tugging at his beard. "It is no secret we all think highly of Miss MacLeod. It is also no secret that the majority of us believe she should be baptized into the Amish faith. I do not say this to single anyone out or to condemn. We must all follow the Lord's leading as we see fit. That is part of our freedom in Christ Jesus. Yet because all of us here, but one, would wholeheartedly bring Miss MacLeod into the church, so we would give our consent and our blessing to a union between her and yourself, Joshua Miller. That being the case, we have asked Pastor Gore to address you both directly since, to be candid, he is the sole impediment to Miss Macleod's inclusion in the Yoder Amish faith, and to a unanimous approval and sanction of your marriage to one another."

Pastor Gore leaned forward in his chair. Kirsten did not see anger or recrimination in his features. Instead, she saw only sadness and a certain sort of warmth, which was as much a surprise to her as the Amish waiting for her and Josh on the front lawn, or the kind way in which they had been welcomed by the bishop and the ministers. "I am not against you, Miss MacLeod. Please understand that. Nor am I against you, Joshua Miller. I see the hand of God on both your lives. It is just that . . . while Miss Macleod may be a woman of peace and righteousness . . . her family has been one of warfare and bloodshed." He held up his hand. "I do not say they lusted to kill. I do not even say they lusted for war. I am sure they did what they felt was right and did it out of what they perceived was a necessity. Nevertheless . . ."

"Before God," Josh interjected.

Kirsten glanced sideways at him.

Pastor Gore stared. "What is that?"

"Before God," Josh repeated. "Kirsten's father, and brother, and fiancé did what they felt was necessary and right before God. They were not simply acting upon their own inclinations. They were acting on what they felt was the will of God for their lives."

Pastor Gore frowned, the old hard wrinkles and lines that Kirsten remembered so well etching themselves into his face once more. "What they believed was God's will, is not what the Yoder Amish believe is God's will. We do not bear arms. Ever."

"I know that, Pastor. But they believed otherwise and acted on their beliefs. Before God. Not before you or I or the Yoder Amish. Before God."

The lines on Pastor Gore's face deepened and sharpened. "That may be. But it does not make them one of us."

"They are not the *Englisch* asking to be brought into the Amish faith. Kirsten is. And she has never borne arms. And never will."

"She must renounce what her father, and brother, and fiancé did."

"What they did before God."

Pastor Gore made a fist and struck the table with it three times. "She must renounce what they did and what they stood for. She must renounce."

"And you would have her defy God Almighty. You would have her break the Ten Commandments."

"What?" Pastor Gore was staggered. "I? I would?"

"What is the Fifth Commandment? What is it, Pastor Gore?"

Pastor Gore did not respond.

"Honor thy father and thy mother," Josh recited softly, *"that thy days may be long upon the land which the Lord thy God giveth thee."* His voice grew even quieter as he looked directly at Pastor Gore. "You would have Kirsten dishonor her father, and what he tried to do before God, on behalf of this country that harbors, and shelters, and defends us. Not only that – you would have Kirsten dishonor her mother as well, for her mother supported her father's decision to join the military, and she prayed for him. They did all this before the face of our holy God and Lord. But you would have Kirsten renounce her parents. You would have her disobey the Lord of heaven and earth, the Lord the Yoder Amish worship and serve, and treat her parents with disdain and contempt. You would have her break the Fifth Commandment. You would. You."

The room was silent.

Kirsten felt as if a great weight was pressing down on her, pressing down on everyone, as if the air itself were stone or lead or thick, black earth. She could hardly breathe or think. For one long minute, she did not look at anyone, but stared at her hands, clasped in her lap and inverted in prayer, the knuckles white, and at the tabletop, at the grain of its wood, at the scratches in its surface, at the circles where hot cups of coffee and spills had left their mark. Her mind was empty. And her heart felt empty as well. Then she heard a strange sound and she looked up.

Pastor Gore's face was disintegrating in a scattering of tears, in trembling lips, in twitches and struggles as he fought to bring his emotions under control. A sound between a cry and a sob came from his throat. He tried several times to speak, but failed. Josh reached across the table and grasped his hand.

"God is here," Josh said. "God is with us. God is love."

"I . . . I . . . would never wish to lead any child of God to break his laws or go against his words," Pastor Gore finally got out. "I would never wish them to break his commandments or dishonor the parents he blessed them with. I . . . did not see. I did not . . . I did not understand. Such a thing is a sin. God knows, I pray that she honors her father and mother, and I pray her days may be long upon the earth, as the Lord has promised those who obey the Fifth Commandment. And I acknowledge she has told us many times that she will not bear arms, and will obey the commandment that follows the one that tells her to honor her parents, the one that says we must not kill, that we must not murder. I know she is committed to the Sixth Commandment, as much as she is committed to the Fifth Commandment. And so . . . and so . . ."

He lapsed into a stream of German words and phrases that Kirsten could not decipher, but she saw the bishop and the other pastors nod. Letting go of Josh's hand, Pastor Gore pushed back his chair and got to his feet. He looked wounded, so wounded that Kirsten's own eyes welled up in sympathy for his pain. He cleared his throat several times.

"I am a proud man," he said. "But not too proud to say I have been wrong, and, in being wrong, have wronged others. I ask for your forgiveness, Miss MacLeod, and your forgiveness, Joshua Miller, and the forgiveness of my brothers here, and the forgiveness of God's people. Above all, it is of our loving God I ask forgiveness and a new beginning. It is of him I ask most of all for love, and mercy, and grace."

"Which he freely and happily gives," Bishop Yoder rumbled. "He is the God of all grace and all peace. In Jesus, he grants you a new life and a new morning. Mercy triumphs over judgment. So it is written."

Pastor Gore looked at Kirsten. "I take back what I have demanded. I take back my insistence that you renounce your father. My dear, I shall permit, I shall permit, oh, my Lord, I shall permit. Before God, join us, my dear girl, and bless us. And as to the marriage, I say, yes, yes, a thousand times yes. Stay with us. Worship God with us. Raise your family among us. Be one with us."

The bishop and other pastors stood.

Yes, they said to the marriage, one after another, *yes, yes, yes.*

Kirsten covered her face with her hands, but the rapid flow of tears passed between her fingers, and down her arms, to the table and the floor. Josh looked at the bishop, he nodded, and Josh placed his arm around Kirsten as she sobbed and shook. In the middle of all this, Pastor Gore suddenly broke into the sunniest smile.

"Now there has been enough sadness," he said. "Now it is time we have a little joy." His smile grew. "Now we have a baptism to look forward to and a wedding after the baptism. Now we must prepare to celebrate. Now we must have days of rejoicing in place of the days of mourning. Now our hearts must dance. Now our souls must sing."

Kirsten had taken her hands from her face, and had seen his smile, the kind of bright, and full, and even humorous smile she had never seen on his face before, and through her tears, she smiled back at him, and the world took on new meaning for her, and the newest sort of hope.

But later, when they were finally alone, Kirsten looked at Josh in astonishment. "And where did all that come from?"

Josh smiled and shrugged with one shoulder. "So, I read it in the Bible."

Chapter 18

December
Sunday afternoon,
the Miller home, 2:07 PM

A gift. A day like this in December is a gift. A gift as good as Christmas.

Kirsten looked down from the third story window at the gathering of people on the back lawn of the Miller house. Set apart from the crowd, Josh stood tall and unmoving in a black suit and white shirt. Next to him, dressed the same way and just as motionless, was Brandon Peters, who would stand with him. They did not speak with anyone. Just waited. In sharp contrast, Josh's nineteen-year-old brother Caleb was wheeling Malachi about in tight, high, tilted-back circles in his wheelchair, and the pair of them found it hilarious. So, Kirsten smiled, the groom and his man were tight and tight-lipped, for an Amish wedding was a serious and holy affair, while his groomsmen were in a mood of hilarity and joy, for an Amish wedding was also a celebration. There was room for both moods today.

"We are not late, not yet." Mrs. Miller was fussing with the hem of the dress she had hand sewn for Kirsten. "How does it feel on you? How are the shoulders?"

"They are fine," Kirsten said, for probably the seventh time. "The dress is beautiful. *Danke schoen,* Mrs. Miller."

"Sarah. You must call me Sarah from now on."

"All right. In any case, you made me an amazing dress and I love the color."

It was a deep and rich navy blue, and it made her think of the way the sky had been in September, when she and Josh had gone to meet with the bishop and pastors. The color of twilight, the peaceful, dreamy color of dusk. The color of miracles, for the night had been a night of miraculous things. The dress brought all that goodness back to her. She loved it.

"I'm grateful the Amish tradition allows me to wear my wedding dress after my marriage," she said to Sarah Miller, still looking down at Josh and Brandon. "The *Englisch* don't do that."

"Ha. Well, it would not be very Amish to make a dress to wear only once in a lifetime, would it? Not very practical. It will be perfect for Sunday worship, and for the baptisms, and weddings you will attend in the years to come. Even the white apron will see use more than once. But we won't speak of that today."

The white organdy apron – Kirsten glanced over to where it lay, neatly draped over a high-backed wooden chair. Such a lovely, and delicate, and translucent cotton weave, as translucent as Huber Run, the rainbow trout stream Josh had shown her in October, and where he promised to camp with her for their three-day honeymoon.

"I will teach you to fly fish," he had told her.

She had wrinkled up her nose. "Oh, the smell of fish. No, thank you."

"Have you ever caught fish?"

"No, and I don't want to either."

"So, you have never smelled fresh trout?"

"Yuck."

"Or eaten any?"

"Double yuck."

"You will change your mind. When you see the beauty of the God-made fish and its colors. When you taste it, after I have stuffed it with corn flakes, and sea salt, and fried it in my cast iron pan with a pat of sweet butter. When you find out that fresh trout smell like the rivers and streams they swim in, and like the smooth stones and sand the water runs over so swiftly, and so perfectly."

"We'll see." Kirsten had folded her arms over her chest. "If the trout and I do not get along, I shall remain in my sleeping bag and nap."

She smiled as she remembered, for she could imagine the trout swimming the length of Huber Run as she gazed at the white apron. But the organdy had been stiffened, where Huber Run flowed like the wind.

"All right then. *Gut*." Sarah Miller stood up, finished with the hem of the blue wedding dress. "Let us get the apron on you."

She gently placed it over Kirsten's head and let it drape over her body. It covered her chest and upper back with white, and fell down almost as far as the length of her dress. Sarah tied it in the back so that it was snug against Kirsten's waist. *The next time someone drapes it over my head, and ties it at the back,* she thought, as Sarah fussed over it, *I shall be dead, for they will bury me in it.*

"So, now your prayer *kapp.*" Sarah removed it from a stand on the dresser. "The next one you wear, when you two go away to Huber Run for your honeymoon, will be black."

"*Vas?*" Kirsten looked at Sarah as the two loose ties of the white *kapp* dangled down over the front of her apron – the *kapp* and apron were both made of the same organdy cotton. "Who told you about Huber Run?"

"Oh, everyone knows, my daughter." Sarah laughed. "The robins and meadowlarks have been busy spreading the news." She adjusted the white *kapp* on Kirsten's head. "Don't worry. No one will bother you on your honeymoon or put crackers in your sleeping bags. We are not the *Englisch* with their silly pranks." She stood back and examined Kirsten's wedding attire with a critical eye. "Besides – who wishes to go out to Huber Run and camp in the middle of December? *Ja,* the weather is fine today, but tomorrow? We could have a blizzard. Only newlyweds would do such a crazy thing. Now if you were to honeymoon in Florida, and spend time with the Amish in Sarasota, and ride around on those recumbent bicycles they favor, and eat oranges and grapefruit under the warm December sun, so then, yes, maybe you would have lots of company. But Huber Run? You should take your ice skates, you will probably need them."

Kirsten laughed. "Or snowshoes."

"Also a good idea. Rebecca joked about you both needing woolen mittens and scarves and parkas."

"Oh, I am for sure taking all of that, she doesn't have to worry." Kirsten glanced out the window again. "I don't see her or the rest of my bridesmaids down below."

"No, they are all waiting for you in the kitchen." Sarah smiled. "Thank you for including her. My goodness, she has not slept in days, she is so excited. And such lovely sky blue dresses your girls are wearing. A perfect complement to your darker color."

"How could I not include Becca? She has always been so sweet to me. And she was practically a matchmaker when it came to Josh and I."

"Ha ha. She says the same thing. *God used me to bring them together. They did not understand what his will was for their lives, but I did.*"

Kirsten grinned. "The lovable imp."

"Always, yes."

Sarah glanced over Kirsten's shoulder and out the window. More Amish were arriving. And not only Amish, but *Englisch* friends of Kirsten, and Brandon, and the Yoder Amish. Nearby, long tables had been set up under the tall pines and were already groaning with hundreds of Amish and *Englisch* dishes.

"Such a day," sighed Sarah. "Such a blessing. In the 50s in December. Just like the day of your baptism. Sunny. Bright. Full of hope."

"Yes." She spotted Pastor Gore, resplendent in perfectly black and perfectly pressed Amish attire. "Yes."

He had been her teacher and mentor as she was taught the ways of the Yoder Amish. Neither he, nor anyone else in leadership, felt she needed a long period of instruction – she had been among them so much and already knew more than many of the Yoder Amish themselves. Two months had been sufficient. The baptism had been in November and, as Sarah had said, the weather had been clear, and clean, and warm, with only a hint of chill from the light northern breezes. They had gone to the riverside where she and Josh had spent so many wonderful hours, the riverside where he had declared his love for her and kissed her for the first time.

Autumn rains had made the river run more quickly than usual and they had stayed close to the bank once they entered it. In other Amish churches, water from the bishop's hands was merely poured over the heads of those being baptized, and it was done in the home where they were worshiping on that particular Sunday. Not so for the Yoder Amish. They not only held to believer's baptism, a baptism undergone by those who were of age and who knew what they were doing – choosing to follow Christ Jesus on the Amish path of their own free will – but they held to full immersion baptism, just as many of their ancestors had undergone in Europe four hundred years before, and been persecuted and killed by other Christians for doing so. Bishop Yoder, as the spiritual leader of the church, and Pastor

Gore, as her instructor in the faith, had waited for her in the river, both wearing hip high fly-fishing waders. She had only worn a plain, and sturdy, and heavy woolen dress that reached to her ankles, one the fast waters would never be able to lift, and had entered the water barefoot, in a sign of simplicity, and humility, and submission to the Lord Jesus Christ, and to the plain and natural Amish way.

The surge had nearly knocked her off her feet. But the bishop and pastor reached out their hands, and held her arms, and steadied her. They asked her a few questions about her faith and she answered the questions appropriately. Then she had shared briefly about her own journey from the *Englisch* to the Amish, and what the Trinity meant to her, and how she wished to walk as Jesus walked and as the Yoder Amish walked. And then they had plunged under the fast, cold waters in the name of the Trinity she had just confessed, and brought her out all wet, and shining, and laughing, and brand new.

She remembered the smiles of Bishop Yoder, and Pastor Gore, and the blessings they spoke over her in the German language. And the smiles from the Amish on the riverbank as well, and the tears, and the hands clasped in prayer and praise, and the singing of a hymn. Several maples had been reluctant to shed their leaves until that Sunday, but now they released them onto the river's surface, where they fastened onto the swift water like drops of blood, and were swept away to the sea. Willows also gave their leaves to the river and – as she believed – to Kirsten too. They gave her their gold, and the promise of a new life, and a new future that had seemed impossible six months before.

"I am Amish." She had lingered in the river, while people waited to help her onto the grassy bank, and whispered the words to herself over and over again. "I am Amish. I am one of the plain folk now, one of the quiet people. I am among those who live in peace and seek it, I am with the women, and children, and men who move about simply in the garden with their God. I am a young woman who lives, and works, and loves with the slow, measured walking pace of a mare or gelding. I am Amish today. I am truly Amish."

And everyone saw the beautiful smile that opened her face to heaven the way a sunflower opened itself to the golden sun in the autumn sky.

"So now I will be married," she said out loud, looking at her husband-to- be in his black suit, still astonished that all of this wonder was really taking place, and was not another one of her fantasies.

"So now you will be married," agreed Sarah, and wrapped an arm around Kirsten's waist. "Now you will be my son's wife. And my daughter. And Rebecca's sister."

"And I will live with Joshua in my parents' home as an Amish bride."

"And he shall be your Amish husband. And we – all of us in the Miller household, and all those among the Yoder Amish – your Amish family."

The sale had been stopped and the furniture returned to the Lancaster home she had grown up in. Electricity had been discontinued and a wood burning stove for cooking and baking moved into the kitchen, while wood burning stoves for heating had been installed in other rooms of the house. Oil lamps and candles had been purchased for lighting. A forge and shop had been built around back for Josh's blacksmithing and farrier work. Stables and a small red barn erected – by the Amish – for the horses and wagons and buggies. They had put up a sturdy clothesline as well and given her a large cloth bag of wooden clothespins. Her world was changing, changing forever, changing into the world she had ached for and longed for, and she relished every day God gave her in it.

"Are you ready?" asked Sarah.

Kirsten took a final look out the window at her Josh, then turned to the woman who would become her second mother, squared her shoulders under the blue dress and white organdy apron, and smiled. "Yes," she said. "I am ready."

Sarah linked an arm through one of Kirsten's. "Then let us begin."

And Kirsten walked across the room, and down the stairs to her smiling bridesmaids, and out the door to the sunshine and the green grass, to Bishop Yoder, and Pastor Gore, and the Yoder Amish, to the tall dark Amish farrier with the blazing blue eyes who was the love of her life, and, her heart racing with a happiness she had never known before, all her beautiful tomorrows.

About the Author

*M*urray Pura was born and raised in Winnipeg, Manitoba, Canada, just north of the Dakotas and Minnesota. His first novel was released in Toronto in 1988 and was a finalist for the Dartmouth Book Award. Since that time, he has published more than a dozen novels, two collections of short stories, and several nonfiction titles. In 2012, he won the Word Award of Toronto for Best Historical Novel for The White Birds of Morning. Murray lives and writes part-time in southwestern New Mexico.

If you enjoyed this story, please leave a review where you purchased this book, or any popular book review site.

For more from this author and MillerWords publishing, please follow us on Facebook:

FB.com/MillerWords

CPSIA information can be obtained
at www.ICGtesting.com
Printed in the USA
LVOW13s0901050818
585990LV00014B/851/P